Cold Dead Cosplay

By

Fiona Angwin

To Katie.

In memory of Fi

Gone to soon

Missed by all who knew her

Richard

Dedication

For all my lovely geeky, nerdy friends, I hope you enjoy it!

Reality Check

The events and central characters in this book are, of course, completely fictional. However, I have included a number of Geek Camp regulars, especially authors, performers and guests, who are an important part of the event. To avoid slowing down the plot I've only used real peoples' names sparingly, and generally only when they are on stage. To find out more about some of the other people, and especially authors, please look at the back of the book where they and some of their works are listed.

How this Book Came About

In 2017 my husband I and went to our first 'Geek Camp', where I was kindly allowed to launch my second novel, Soul-Scars. Since then I've been to every event, Samantha Lee Howe and David J Howe (Telos Publishing Ltd) have just published my most recent novel 'Hunted by Demons', I've created my Sci-Fi Puppet Show 'Behind The Sofa' FOR the event and now I've just written this novella 'Cold Dead Cosplay' set AT the event. I think things may have spiralled out of control!

Acknowledgements

They say it takes a village to raise a child, and it certainly took quite a few members of my Geek Camp family to complete the final details of this book. To everyone who allowed me to pester them for information, photographs for the cover or permission to include them in the book, thank you.

These include Samantha Lee Howe, David J Howe, James King, Kirsty Brown, Mark, Angie and Saskia Estlea, Andy Gray, Roger Chard, Donna Stacey, Joanne R'rith, Chris Beard, Iain Shaw, John Jurgen Hudson, Andy Lyth and Rebecca Townley.

Special thanks to Ady Wilce for doing a whole photoshoot for me as Ramilid, and to Adam Colclough for letting me weave him through this story as the Host.

Thanks also to Martin Nelson for editing and formatting the book for me, and Peter Jeffrey-Bourne (Dan) for creating the brilliant cover, and of course Richard Angwin, for putting up with being dragged along to Geek Camp time after time.

Photography Credits for the cover

Image: Ramilid – The Dark Elf
Photographer: Ady Wilce
Cosplayer: Ady Wilce

Image: The Joker/The Host
Photographer: Simon Dunkerley
Cosplayer: Adam Colclough

Image: The Hobbit
Photographer: Roger Chard
Cosplayer: Jessica Phantomhievu

Image: Thrandiel & Nimue
Photographer: Mortin Comber
Cosplayers: Mairion Oakley
                      Wolfka Maria Redway

Image: Lady Loki
Photographer: Richard Angwin
Cosplayer: Rebecca Townley

Image: Crow
Photographer: Roger Chard

Photographers mentioned in the book
In Order of appearance

Roger Hathaway: Greenscreen Photographer

The only non-Geek Camp person I've smuggled in, but we have had greenscreen photoshoots sometimes and I know him and his work from other events. His company is Roger Hathaway Photography

Simon Dunkerley: Red Spektor and SD Photography

Karen Woodham: Blazing Minds Website

Chapter One

Jamie groaned as the bright sunlight forced its way in between his eyelids. He clamped them shut and twisted in the bed, trying to bury his head in the pillow.

'Why do I always do this?' he wondered to himself. 'Drink so much on the first night of the event that I'm wasted before things even get off the ground.' Still, it had been so good to see everyone again - to spend a loud and crazy night with like-minded people. The kind of crowd who really understood him, who cared about the same type of things.

He heard the sound of several pairs of boots marching along the path outside his caravan, and grinned. Torn between reluctance to open his eyes and exacerbate his hangover and a desire to see what was going on, he sat up in bed, lifted the curtain away from the window to peer out, and smiled.

The orcs were practicing their drill on the way over to the training ground. Despite the fact that the noise they were making was causing his head to explode, and the light bouncing off their shields was painful to look at, he couldn't help enjoying the spectacle in front of him.

'Only at a Sci-Fi Convention,' he thought, with a grin. He scrambled out of bed losing his balance as the sheets got caught around his legs. He smashed down onto the pile of luggage which he'd dumped in the corner the night before and began to panic about whether he'd broken anything. It had taken him months to create his cosplays for this event and he was far more worried about damaging them than himself. As he climbed back onto his feet his head began to spin again, and he decided he needed a shower before he could face checking his outfits.

An hour later Jamie was feeling - well, not bright eyed and bushy tailed, perhaps - but several degrees better than he had when he'd woken up. The shower had helped, of course, and so had finding out that he hadn't done any lasting damage to his cosplays when he fell on them. With his light brown hair still wet from the shower, and his blue eyes a *little* less blurry than they had been, he wondered into the kitchen area to make himself a coffee. The friends he was sharing the caravan with were pouring over the event programme at breakfast, all trying to decide which interviews, panels and entertainments they were going to try to get to. There was always so much going on that it was almost impossible to fit it all in, and they agreed to split up and go to whatever appealed to each of them the most, and then meet up for a drink together later in the day.

Of course, before they could set off anywhere, they had to help each other get into their various cosplays. Only Artie didn't bother to dress up over the weekend, claiming he preferred to be comfortable in old jeans and a geeky tee-shirt, after wearing a suit all week, but he was happy to help everyone else as they strapped on various elements of their cosplays. To be fair, he was one of those men who looked good in anything he wore, being tall and thin with dark brown eyes that contrasted strangely with his pale, almost platinum blond hair which fell across his forehead in an unruly fringe.

'Just call me The Dresser,' Artie joked as he tightened the laces on Emily's corset. Jamie looked on jealously, wishing he'd had the nerve to offer. He'd had a soft spot for Emily for the last two years, ever since her then boyfriend Rex had brought her along to the event. Their relationship had ended soon afterwards, but Emily kept coming to the Conventions. She had fallen in love with Sci-Fi, with Cosplay, with the atmosphere - but not, unfortunately, with Jamie. Not, of course, that she knew how he felt about her, because he hadn't had the nerve to tell her. The only time they spent together was at Sci-Fi Conventions, and as they could only afford go to a handful each year - well, progress was slow.

The other two members of the group were Luke and Katy. They were a couple who shared a passionate love for each other, and Dr Who. Their cosplays generally reflected that, and for this event, Luke had created a Dalek and Katy was dressed as Osgood. Jamie couldn't help thinking that Katy, in her lab coat and trailing stripy scarf, with her dark brown haired pulled back in a ponytail, and her hazel eyes peering out through Osgood style black framed glasses, would have a much more comfortable time than Luke in his heavy Dalek outfit. It was made from foam panels, each accurately decorated with roundels and bound together by straps. The whole ensemble had been sprayed silver and the effect was fantastic. Still, Jamie wouldn't have wanted to be trapped inside it all day - although the dome at the top was hinged so Luke could flip it back to watch things properly or take a breather when he wanted to. Jamie suspected that Luke, who was getting ever so slightly plump, had chosen a cosplay that deliberately hid his body, though he really didn't need to. Geek Camp was a very uncritical place. They all agreed that Luke looked quite amusing with his redhaired head sticking out of the open dome, and his green eyes sparkling with excitement. Actually, the whole group was excited; they'd been looking forward to the event for months.

Jamie had made a real effort this year, which he was hoping would impress Emily. He'd gone for wearing his simpler outfit for the first day of the event and was dressed as Bilbo Baggins - alright, not exactly sci-fi, but fantasy was accepted too - and was saving his showier cosplay for the second day. This time he was determined to enter the Cosplay Competition, which always took place on the second full day of the event.

Jamie's Bilbo cosplay was fairly basic, with a lot of the clothing found in charity shops, but it suited him, since he was on the skinny side, and not especially tall. He had bought a good quality wig, slightly pointed ears and slip-on hobbit feet. His pride and joy - chosen to complete the outfit, was the Arkenstone - which Jamie had tucked into his pocket.

Of course, in The Hobbit, the Arkenstone was a precious gem, guarded by the dragon Smaug inside the Lonely Mountain, and searched for by Thorin Oakenshield, King under the Mountain and leader of the company of dwarves. Thorin was unaware that the hobbit had already found and claimed it for himself, and the Arkenstone played an important part in the development of the story.

Originally Jamie had been looking on-line for a ring, a replica of Gollum's 'precious', but then he's spotted this beautiful stone, and he couldn't resist it. Since it was for sale on ebay, he'd had to bid for it, and had ended up spending much more than he could afford, but there was something about it that really attracted him.....and it was certainly more original to complete his outfit than a ring would have been.

He meant to get out the stone to show it to Emily, but he was too busy just then admiring her cosplay. She'd gone for a steampunk look, with a corset, layered mid-length Victorian style skirt and long boots, all topped off with a veiled top hat with goggles fixed to it. Her long blond hair hung in curls that were, rather unusually, natural, and a broad smile danced beneath her light blue eyes. Jamie thought she looked stunning. Mind you, Jamie thought she looked stunning when she was chilling out in the caravan in Winnie the Pooh pyjamas, so he had to admit he was just a tiny bit biased.

Just as they were all about to set off, Artie grabbed Jamie by the arm.

'I've got something for you,' he said to his friend, 'For your stone. When you showed it to me last night, I thought it was a shame for you to have such a great prop, and just keep it in your pocket all day, so I made you this.' Artie pulled out a little oval cage, made from twisted copper wire, and hanging from a leather cord. 'Now you can slot the Arkenstone into this and wear it.'

'That's brilliant,' said Jamie gratefully. The stone holder was quite detailed, and Artie had obviously spent a lot of the previous night working on it. Jamie was touched.

'I didn't know you could make things,' he said. 'You never do cosplay.'

'I just don't enjoy dressing up,' replied Artie, 'But I love making things. I didn't bring any materials with me though, so I had to scrounge the copper wire from Luke's toolbox, and Emily supplied the cord.'

'Happy to help,' added Emily with a grin. Jamie grinned back, delighted that Emily had contributed to the gift. He slotted the stone into the cage, and Artie twisted a tiny catch he'd built into the device, to stop it from slipping out, then the five of them set off for the main venue, to watch the official opening.

Their walk took them between the caravans, and on towards an open area near the different venues. One of the things everyone loved about this particular sci-fi convention was that it was based in a holiday park, with accommodation you could hire, and all the activities were close together. There were several venues for the various activities, and plenty of stalls selling all kinds of sci-fi and steampunk items. Best of all, in Artie's opinion were the book stalls. Some were manned by indie authors selling their own books, but the biggest – The Book Base - was run by a publishing firm that helped organise the event each year. Artie was tempted to rush straight there, but he resisted. He'd go to the opening event first, with his friends.

Their walk took a little longer than planned as they kept stopping, either to greet friends from previous events, or to show off their cosplays to strangers asking to take their photos. Chatting to total strangers was part of the event's vibe, and nobody ever objected to being stopped for a photo or being asked how they made some element of their cosplay.

****

Chapter Two

The group of friends were so busy with these 'normal' activities that they didn't notice something less usual – they were being watched by a creature lurking in the bushes. To be honest, the creature didn't really need to hide. Nobody would have thought twice about seeing a strange supernatural being wandering around in broad daylight. Not at Geek Camp. But old habits die hard, and the creature was very, very old.

His name was Ramilid, a dark elf, creature of moonlight and Enforcer of the Unseelie Court, and he was there on business.

'Is that him?' Ramilid asked the miserable human crouching beside him. Simon nodded.

'I think so,' he whispered. 'It's one of them anyway. I've never met him. J.S. Patterson paid by PayPal and I sent him the stone by post, but that's one of the names registered to the caravan that group are staying in.' He risked a glance up to his captor. 'You're not going to … kill him, are you? He hasn't done anything wrong – just a bit of on-line shopping.'

'Unlike you and your friends,' replied Ramilid, giving the man a rather unpleasant smile. 'You definitely earned your punishment. Digging up the Hoard of the Fae and selling it. Your friends deserved to die … and so do you!'

****

Simon tried to blink back the images of what had happened the night before. He and his friends Eddy and Maureen had been celebrating their success. After finding a small hoard of old coins and strange objects with their metal detectors they had decided not to hand them over to the Coroner, as they were supposed to, but to sell all the items on-line and split the profits. The first three sales had gone well, and no government officials had come knocking at their door, so they'd got together over a few drinks and agreed to start listing the rest of the items.

Their treasures were piled up on the coffee table in the middle of Simon's sitting room, and Maureen was photographing them and trying to find interesting ways to describe each object so that it could be listed for sale. Simon was at the computer logging into his ebay account and Eddy was topping up the drinks. At that moment life as he knew it ceased for Simon. He heard a crash as his front door was smashed to fragments, and a furious looking – thing – strode into the room.

Taller than any of them, the creature looked like a cross between a character from a Tolkien movie, and something out of a horror film. He stood in the middle of the room, dripping menace. He held a long, dark staff, which had some kind of ovoid, surrounded by scales, at the top of it.

'Who are you?' stammered Simon. 'What are you doing in my house?'

'Retrieving the property of the Unseelie Court,' the figure replied, 'And punishing you for its theft.'

'Theft,' spluttered Eddy, as he choked on his beer. 'You're having a laugh. We haven't stolen anything.'

The creature thrust his staff crosswise at Eddy, pinning him to the wall by the throat. Simon tried to make sense of what he was seeing. The bearded figure had long dark hair, was dressed in sombre clothing, which was layered and shaped like armour, and seemed to shimmer the more you looked at it. Simon couldn't decide if it was black or dark green or midnight blue. His skin was slightly iridescent too, though paler than his clothing. Simon had thought at first that the creature was wearing a cloak, but as the figure turned to attack Eddy he realised that the dusky trailing shapes weren't fabric but some kind of wings, skin-thin and gleaming darkly, like the carapace of a beetle.

COLD DEAD COSPLAY

'You're a fairy!' stated Maureen, shocked.

'Oh, yes. Did you think we were those glittery little creatures you see in old picture books? How wrong you are.' Since that was exactly what the three humans in the room thought fairies were – in addition to being imaginary – there was nothing they could say. Eddy couldn't have spoken anyway, with the staff crushing his throat.

'I don't understand,' said Simon, while Maureen leapt forward and attempted to hit the creature over the head with an empty beer bottle, in an effort to rescue Eddy. The fairy retaliated by flinging her across the room with such force that she smashed into a wall and fell to the floor, her neck twisted at an awkward angle. She screamed as the blow struck her, and groaned as she hit the floor, then there was silence. Deathly silence.

Simon leapt out of his chair towards her but felt some force holding him back.

'Don't bother, you won't be able to do anything for her. I fear I let her off too easily for the offence committed – a quick and almost painless death – but she was trying to rescue her friend, and even the dark Fae recognise loyal friendship as a virtue deserving some measure of respect.'

'You showed her respect by killing her?' spluttered Simon.

'Indeed,' replied the creature. 'And you two will shortly discover just how kind I have been, when I give you *your* due punishment. I'm Ramilid, by the way, since you were polite enough to ask my name. I wouldn't normally offer it to a human - there is a power in names - but as you will both be dead shortly...' Ramilid shrugged.

'Please let Eddy go,' begged Simon, trying to sound calm and reasonable. 'You're choking him.'

Ramilid stepped away from the wall leaving his staff, which somehow stayed in position and continued to pin Eddy in place. The creature seemed to be exerting some kind of power over them both, preventing either of them from moving.

The dark elf wandered over to the coffee table and began to inspect the treasures piled on it, picking up piece after piece and examining each in turn, before putting them into a dark leather bag that was hung over his shoulder. Simon and Eddy watched, silent except for the guttural sounds Eddy was making as he struggled to breathe, the staff still pushing crossways against his throat.

Now that the creature was closer to him Simon saw that there was a dead beetle apparently clinging to the dark elf's ear. At least he hoped that the beetle was dead. The idea that the little bug would choose to hang there if it was alive seemed particularly weird. When the table was clear Ramilid spun on his heels looking from Simon to Eddy and back.

'Where are the other three items? Three of the treasures are missing. The stone, the silver wreath and the chalice. Where have you hidden them?'

'We haven't hidden them,' said Simon. 'We sold them – on ebay – we didn't know anyone owned them.'

'Even by human law you knew that hidden treasures were not yours to buy and sell. You have no defence. No human law will protect you from the vengeance of the Unseelie Court.' Ramilid looked at the two men, considering his choice. 'Who sold the items?' the dark elf whispered.

'Me,' Simon whispered in reply. He expected to be thrown across the room, like Maureen, to be dead within moments. Instead Ramilid turned on Eddy, saying 'Then I have no need of you.' A cold smile crossed his face. 'I believe you humans think that fairies form allegiances with certain animals. Some of us do, but don't be thinking we'd choose anything cute and furry. The dark elves have – other tastes.' He clicked his fingers and the room filled with crows, swooping through the smashed front door and into the living room. Simon tried to cower away from them as they battered against his face, but he couldn't move. Ramilid pointed a finger at Eddy and suddenly all the birds began to attack his friend, flying in close to peck at his face with their sharp beaks, and tear at his body with their claws. Eddy started to scream, and carried on screaming, and Simon found himself wailing in sympathy and in horror, but there was nothing he could do to protect his friend.

After several minutes Eddy was a faceless, ravaged mess ... no longer moving, or whimpering, and when Ramilid eventually removed the staff that had held him against the wall, Eddy's body slumped to the floor. Simon expected the birds to attack *him* next, but instead the elf clicked his fingers and the feathered killers flew out of the room.

Suddenly Simon found himself free from whatever force or enchantment had been holding him in place and half ran, half crawled across the room to see if there was anything he could do for his friend, but Eddy was beyond help. The state of the body, with its eyeballs pecked out, leaving just bloodied empty eye sockets, and nothing recognisable about the face, was so horrific that Simon passed out, and the world went blank for a while.

****

Chapter Three

The largest venue at Geek Camp, nicknamed the Star Base for the weekend, was filling up for the opening event. Those who weren't too hungover, or who hadn't partied the previous night away, tried to get there in plenty of time to get a seat. Melissa and her friend Jess were trying to save five seats between the two of them, which was fine while the space was half empty, but increasingly difficult as more people arrived.

'Where have they got to?' Mel hissed, but all Jess could do was shrug.

'They said they were meeting us here,' Mel continued. 'We agreed we'd mainly stick together. Our cosplays work best *together*.' This group of friends had gone for a fantasy theme, dressing as characters from The Lord of the Rings, although one of them had gone for a character from The Hobbit instead. Melissa had chosen to be Galadriel, Lady of Lothlórien, The Lady of the Woods. She'd adapted a second-hand wedding dress, with a slim, elegant line, adding layers of silver and white lace over it. She was really pleased with the effect, even if she had had to resort to gluing some of the lace into position when she ran out of sewing time. She'd bought a long silvery wig which fell in loose ringlets all the way down her back. It was long enough to sit on, which turned out to be a little awkward as if she wasn't careful when she moved it could tug backwards off her head. She'd considered trimming it, but it looked so good it seemed a shame to shorten it. The only other hitch was that the wig was so full she couldn't keep it tucked behind her pointed ears, so they were hidden most of the time. Melissa had also bought gardening wire to make herself a silver ring and crown, but after battling pointlessly with trying to shape the wire for several evenings, she decided that jewellery making wasn't her skill set.

She had been running out of time, so she'd gone onto ebay and that was where she'd found the beautiful silver-metal crown. It wasn't exactly like the one in the photos from the film adaptation, but it was pretty close. It should be, for the price she'd paid for it. She'd had to pay for first class postage as well, to have a chance of it reaching her in time. As it was, she'd forced everyone to wait for it to arrive before they'd set off for Geek Camp yesterday, which hadn't gone down too well with the others. Even Jess, who was her closest friend, had become a bit fed up with the delay, as it meant they didn't arrive at the site until the evening, and had missed the quiz by the time they'd found their caravan, unloaded the car and got themselves organised to go out for the night.

The quiz was always a fun, if rather confusing, start to the event, partly because you had to be *really* geeky to even understand most of the questions, and partly because the Host for the event often forgot to provide enough (or any) pens, leaving everyone scrambling around in bags and pockets to be able to take part. It was now a Thing to be able to pull out a whole packet of pens to present to the Host to share round. Jess had bought a packet especially for the purpose, so she was particularly keen to get to the quiz, and particularly hacked off when she couldn't.

Still, all that was forgotten when Jess saw Melissa in her Galadriel cosplay, with the beautiful crown on her gloriously bewigged head. Jess had sighed, partly in admiration and partly with jealousy. She herself had chosen to cosplay Arwen, daughter of Elrond. Her character was half elven but gave up her immortality to marry Aragorn and eventually die with him. Jess loved the romance of it, and had enthusiastically added flowing, trumpet shaped sleeves of silver fabric to an old long blue velvet dress, she even bought a full-length grey velvet cloak to complete the look.

Her own hair was long and dark, which was a perfect foil to Mel's appearance, and she'd left it loose, though tucked behind her synthetic elfin shaped ears. However, standing beside her best friend in front of the mirror that morning two things had struck her. The first was that Arwen was meant to be really beautiful and she, Jess, wasn't.

Pleasant looking yes, but not beautiful ... and standing next to Mel she felt positively plain.

Jess's mother always said that "beauty is in the eye of the beholder" and told her daughter to be grateful for her long lashes and dark brown eyes, but Jess wasn't convinced. A quirky smile couldn't compete with her best friend's beauty, because even without her cosplay, Melissa was beautiful.

The other thing that struck Jess was that the dress she'd adapted was terribly revealing. She'd tweaked the neckline down to match the one worn by her character in the film, and now she saw herself in it she realised that she'd cut it really low. Much lower than anything Jess would wear normally. Could she really hang around all day in that? In public?

One of the things Jess loved about cosplay was that it gave her confidence, usually. She was often rather shy, and felt nervous amongst big crowds of people, but being a character was like having a mask to hide behind. It made her feel safer, more out-going. On this occasion, however, worrying about the cut of her dress, while sitting in the Star Base surrounded by people, Jess was feeling even more self-conscious than usual.

'Are you sure you don't have any scraps of lace left? I just need enough to pin across the front, to cover my cleavage.'

'You don't have much of a cleavage,' Mel giggled, 'And I don't have any lace left. I didn't bring any fabric at all, just some glue and a needle and thread for repairs.'

Jess glanced down at her admittedly rather flat chest and sighed. She wrapped her cloak tightly around herself, covering up her dress almost completely, and looked around the space, wondering again where their friends had got to.

****

COLD DEAD COSPLAY

Alec, Mike and Lee had run into Jamie and his friends as they all walked towards the venue. Lee, being shorter than Mike and Alec, had chosen to cosplay as Thorin Oakenshield, and as soon as he saw Jamie dressed as Bilbo Baggins, he hurried over brandishing a hefty oak branch.

'How dare you flaunt my Arkenstone before my very eyes?' said Lee in a threatening manner. 'Return to me that which is mine by right!'

Of course, Lee and Jamie had never met before, but it seemed perfectly reasonable to step into role play when they were dressed as characters from the same story.

'I claim this stone as my due,' replied Jamie, 'My share of the treasure, as promised, in return for my duties as Burglar on your behalf.'

The two groups of friends merged as they admired each other's outfits. Lee was really proud of his work on the Thorin cosplay. He'd made the surcoat from scratch, adding half sleeves and decorating it with braid and a broad faux fur collar which reached down the full length of the surcoat to the hem. Best of all he'd created his own leather gauntlets, fingerless of course, to allow the dwarf to fight in battles. A gold chain, a long wig, a beard and the oak branch completed the look.

'Did you make those gauntlets yourself?' came the muffled voice of Luke, from inside the Dalek. 'They're awesome.'

'Nice touch with the oak branch,' added Emily.

'Easier to carry than a shield,' agreed Lee, 'And it's true to the book. In an early battle Thorin's shield broke, and he picked up an oak branch to use as a shield...'

'**And so, he became known as Thorin Oakenshield**.' Almost everyone chimed in to finish Lee's story. It was well enough known after all.

'Plus,' Lee added, 'I can carry it like a weapon, without breaking the rules.'

They all nodded. Real weapons, or even ones that looked too realistic, were never allowed into conventions, for obvious reasons, but those rules did give cosplayers all kinds of challenges if they were to complete their character without breaking any of them.

Mike's Legolas, Prince of Mirkwood, cosplay was admired. He'd bought that and the long blond wig online, but they were really good quality, with moulded plastic sections on the tunic and boot tops to mimic the costume Orlando Bloom wore in the film. He'd only needed to add a cloak and elf ears, and his cosplay was complete. He'd have loved to carry a longbow and arrows, but rules were rules.

Artie wandered over to Alec, who was slightly older than the rest of them, and was standing a little to one side, looking nervous, to introduce himself.

'Elrond, Lord of Rivendell?' he asked looking at the older man's costume.

'Yes,' Alec replied with a grin. 'I wasn't sure anyone would get it. Most of it is put together from charity shop finds. I was lucky enough to come across an old full-length embroidered dressing gown and then altered the sleeves and collar. The cloak is cut from an old curtain. Is it ok? I've not done a full-on cosplay before.'

'It's terrific! Of course, it's ok! And anything goes in cosplay, that's the fun of it,' said Artie.

'This long wig isn't very comfortable though, and my crown keeps slipping.' Jamie joined them to admire the twisted silver wreath around Alec's head.

'Where did you get the crown?' Jamie asked enviously. 'It looks fantastic! It must have cost a fortune.'

'Yes,' Alec groaned. 'I found it online, and I was running out of time, so I went for it.' The older man turned and looked at Artie with a puzzled expression. 'I'm sorry, I can't work out who you're cosplaying?' Artie burst out laughing.

'I'm not.' Artie chuckled, 'I'm just me. Artie.'

'Pleased to me you, Artie,' said Alec, and they all began to move on together, heading for the Star Base.

'We'll have missed the opening,' Emily announced.

'No, we won't,' said Katy, hurrying on ahead. 'With a bit of luck, they'll be running late. We won't be able to find any seats though.'

Mike, Lee and Alec looked at each other in horror, realising that Mel and Jess had been up there waiting for them for ages – and was certain Melissa would be in a bit of a mood over it. All eight of them strode towards the venue together, though Luke in his Dalek, struggled to keep up.

****

Chapter Four

Still hiding in the bushes Ramilid cursed. During the banter about 'The Arkenstone' when the two groups met, the dark elf had seen that it was indeed the stone he was looking for – though Arkenstone was not it's true Fae name. However, it was a stone of power, giving strength to and enhancing the abilities of whoever possessed it. Not that the foolish young man wearing it looked like he had any abilities to enhance. The other item they were searching for was going to be harder to identify.

Simon knew the silver wreath had also been sold to someone attending this event, because they had messaged him to request, he get the item in the post quickly so that it reached them before they set off for it. The trouble was he didn't have a name, so he couldn't pin down who it was out of a couple of thousand people at the event, and the address he'd sent it to was a click and collect pick up point in a town. The payment had been by direct transfer, so they had his account details, but he didn't have theirs.

He knew that Ramilid was only keeping him alive until he had retrieved the objects from the Hoard. Then he'd be destroyed just like his friends. Simon remembered coming to in his living room, with his friends sprawled dead on the floor. Ramilid had been crouched over Eddy's ravaged body – there was blood on the elf's lips, and Simon could have sworn that the edges of the creature's dark wings were tinged with deepest red, which they hadn't been before. Simon threw up over the carpet and kept throwing up until his stomach was empty. Which may have made his body feel a little better, but his brain was still screaming. These were his friends, dead in front of him. He had been powerless to protect them, or himself; in his heart he knew he'd end up dead too. It was just going to take a little longer, which seemed worse somehow.

Ramilid had hauled Simon to his feet insisting that he assist the elf in locating the three missing objects. Since all the information was in the computer, which Ramilid didn't know how to use, Simon had to go into his ebay and email accounts to find the details.

'The chalice won't have been delivered to its new owner yet,' whispered Simon, looking at the screen. 'It'll still be in the post. I only sent it yesterday – second class.' Actually, he'd used first class post, but he hoped the lie would buy the purchaser a little more time and give him a chance to try and stop this creature. Even as he thought it, he knew he was kidding himself. He didn't think there was any way he could stop Ramilid.

'Start with the wreath and the stone then. Where did they end up?'

Simon remembered being surprised when he'd first realised from the messages that he'd received two of the objects had been sold to different people but were going to end up at the same event. Perhaps it wasn't so surprising though. Both items would appeal to people who were into cosplay, and they were sold just before a really big cosplay event at the point when people were stressing about finishing off their cosplays and realising they'd run out of time to make the last few accessories.

Simon stood up at his laptop to grab a pen and paper and jot down the addresses Ramilid was demanding, which gave him a few seconds when the screen was masked by his body to send an email. It was pretty incoherent … along the lines of: -

Help! Weird Killer - kidnapped – Geek Camp

 He sent a copy to his own address in case the police searched his computer, and to his friend Bella, the only person who might just take it seriously. He managed to tap the 'mark as urgent' symbol and pressed send just as Ramilid came to look over his shoulder. Thankfully Simon managed to shut the lid of the laptop before the elf saw what he'd written, but he wasn't sure if the email had sent before closing the lid had switched the device off.

The dark elf looked Simon up and down and shook his head.

'I can't take you with me like that. It will arouse curiosity. Also, you smell. Wash.' Ramilid dragged Simon upstairs and shoved him into the bathroom. Simon felt oddly thankful to be able to wash away his friends' blood, but he expected to be covered in his own very soon.

He was pretty sure there was only one way this was going to end, for him anyway.

****

Now that Ramilid could see all the convention goers making their way towards the venue, he realised that he *could* actually hide in plain sight. If anything, his captive looked more out of place than he did. Although lots of people didn't join in with the cosplay, they all looked relaxed, as they were enjoying the event. Simon, on the other hand, was a jabbering wreck, shaking with fear and still in shock. There were even a few deep cuts and scratches from the crows' attack marking his face. Perhaps they'd have to stay out of sight after all. The other problem Ramilid could see was that there were a lot of crowns and wreaths on peoples' heads. The stone he had recognised, for he had seen it once, long ago, and could sense its power, but the silver wreath? That he'd never seen, and so far, hadn't sensed. Getting it back was going to be harder than he'd expected. Harder for whoever got in his way, at least.

Ramilid was tempted to kill Simon, just to get rid of him, but he wanted to be sure he had all three objects back before he did so. The pathetic young man was better at navigating the modern world than the dark elf, so he'd have to hold onto him. For now.

He hauled Simon to his feet and shook him by the shoulders to get his attention. He was glazing over again.

'Can you see the wreath? You found it. You sold it. You should be able to recognise it. Have you seen it yet?'

COLD DEAD COSPLAY

Simon shook his head, trying to focus. So many of the passing cosplayers were wearing some kind of headdress. He could rule of a lot of the sci-fi cosplayers. They looked amazing, but the item he'd sold didn't suit their chosen characters.

'We are going to walk alongside these - these - mortals, and you are going to help me find the wreath you stole. If you try to speak to anyone, or to run away, I will kill you. Do you doubt me?'

Simon shook his head. He didn't doubt Ramilid for an instant.

'Once we have located the second item we can decide on when and how to retrieve them. I don't want to arouse anyone's curiosity by reclaiming the stone before finding the wreath. Now come. And try to look ... normal.'

Simon dreaded to think how this creature planned to 'retrieve' the objects and hoped it wouldn't involve killing the people who'd bought them. If it did their blood would be on his head.

As they walked along with the crowd, Simon scanned the people around him, searching for anything that might be the missing wreath. He was amazed to see the top of a sousaphone up ahead; the rest of it wrapped around a man clad in a red and black Deadpool cosplay, but with a red cap and black mask instead of a full-face hood. Friends of the man were calling out hello and referring to him as Trumpetpool. A tiny bit of Simon's brain was enjoying the distraction of the incredible spectacle surrounding him. The rest of it was screaming for an escape route, but Ramilid held him tightly by the arm and there was nowhere he could go.

****

.

Chapter Five

Bella had raced around to Simon's house on the outskirts of Witney as soon as she'd opened the email, he'd sent her, only to find the place surrounded by police. A neighbour had alerted them early that morning, having seen the smashed front door. Thankfully the neighbour had been too nervous to walk into the building, so they wouldn't have to live with the image that confronted the police team when they'd entered the room.

Inspector Blake Hornchurch of the Thames Valley Police was glad for the woman concerned. He'd rather he hadn't had to see the devastation himself. The woman's body was no worse than many he'd come across, but the man's – that was something else. Blake didn't even want to think about what had the power to do that to someone, let alone why.

The Scenes of Crime Officers were working their way through the room, which on this occasion was a pretty challenging task, when Bella reached the front door and demanded to see Simon. Hearing her loud, insistent voice outside Inspector Hornchurch went to find out who was making a fuss, and why they sounded so panicked. The uniformed officer on the door had wisely not told the young woman anything except that she couldn't enter, which was useful as it gave Blake a chance to assess her for himself. She was young, to him anyway, in her early twenties, with wild blond hair and dark grey eyes. Her clothes looked like she'd dragged them on in a hurry, which she had, as soon as she'd opened the email.

'Where's Simon?' she demanded. 'Is he alright? I got his email. It frightened me.'

Bella looked the inspector up and down, as if trying to decide whether to trust him. He looked about mid-thirties, with mousey brown hair which seemed to be cut – occasionally – for neatness, not for style, and was wearing a slightly worn black suit. He was getting wrinkles

29

round his eyes, the sort people usually got from smiling, although at that moment he was gazing at her sharply. She decided that he looked kind, and she could trust him. She found the message in her smart phone and passed it to the inspector.

'I found this when I opened my emails this morning. That's why I came round. Is Simon here? Is he alright?'

Blake sighed. He hated breaking bad news, and it was often better to keep details under wraps for as long as possible, but if this girl could shed any light on the situation it could save them precious time, and in a murder investigation time was invaluable. They'd already identified the property as belonging to a Simon Potts, but whether he was the male body in the room, or the killer, they didn't know yet. Forensics officers were searching the corpses for identification. The word kidnap in the email made him wonder though. Perhaps there was a third explanation. He hoped so, anyway. He really didn't relish telling this young lady that her friend was either dead or a murderer.

****

By the time The Lord of the Rings group of cosplayers had reached the Star Base with their new friends it was standing room only and the opening ceremony was just beginning. The entertainment team were up on the stage performing acrobatic dances to sci-fi theme tunes; and anyone in a bulky cosplay was already feeling hot.

Mel and Jess had been straining around looking for their friends for ages and had eventually given up saving seats for them. Now the two girls made their way over to join the group.

'Where have you been?' demanded Melissa. 'We've been waiting ages.'

'Sorry,' said Mike, and began to introduce the girls to their new friends. It was one of the things everybody loved about Geek Camp. You'd make new friends each time you went, and would often keep in touch with them in between, on social media at least, and search them out at the next event. It was a bit like being part of an ever-extending family.

Alec was looking at Jess. She looked stunning as Arwen, to him, anyway, though he wasn't quite sure why, soon after she'd joined them, she'd blushed and begun to hold her cloak closed at the front quite so tightly, hiding what he thought was a beautiful dress. It was Mel who had suggested to Alec that he should cosplay as Elrond, and he'd enjoyed creating all the elements of his outfit, but he felt a bit uncomfortable about cosplaying as Jess's father. He really did like her - though not in a fatherly way at all - and now it struck him that his character choice just emphasised the age difference between them. He worked with Mike at a small IT firm and it was Mike who'd introduced him to the rest of the group, and to Geek Camp. They all lived near enough each other to meet up for a drink occasionally, or to go to the cinema together as a group, and he kept thinking about asking Jess out on a date. Then he'd look in a mirror, remind himself that he was twelve years older than her, and forget it. Now their respective cosplay choices made it seem even less possible. He was afraid she'd think of him as some old pervert.

They all turned to concentrate on the stage, joining in with the cheering and shouting as the guests for the event were confirmed and one or two unexpected special appearances were announced. Then there were a few minutes of set up time before the first interview of the day which was with Andrew Lee Potts from Primeval; and the friends consulted the event program and decided who was going to which sessions.

Geek Camp was packed full of interviews with actors and actresses who'd been in some of the top Sci-Fi and Fantasy films and series over the years, as well as directors, puppeteers, and writers who all had fascinating stories to tell. In addition, there were entertainments scattered across several stages, as well as author panels and prop-making sessions and demonstrations by those who drew comic strips and made remarkable objects for stage and screen.

And then there were the books. Lots of lovely books from the genres that most appealed to the people who came to Geek Camp. And lots of opportunities to meet the authors and chat to them. Some were really well known, while others were new, but all were welcome. Plenty of traders came to the event too, selling Sci-Fi Collectables, Steampunk items and more, and nearly everyone who came to Geek camp went home clutching a new stash of goodies.

Luke and Katy had already decided to head over to the second venue, called the Moon Base, so that they could get a seat for Pop-Up Puppets who had their new show on in about half an hour.

'If we don't go now, we'll never get a seat,' said Katy, with a grin. Not that Luke would be able to sit down. Not inside his Dalek. Still, he'd been getting some extremely positive comments about it, which made up for the discomfort somewhat.

****

The inspector had spared Bella as many details about what had happened in Simon's house as possible, but she'd still learned enough to know that there were two dead bodies, although the police now knew that neither of them were Simon's, and that something truly horrific had occurred. Once she was told the names of the two victims, she explained that they were Simon's detectorist friends. She knew they'd had a find recently, and Simon was very excited about it, but she didn't know a lot more than that, as she hadn't seen any of the objects. She'd been away visiting her family for the last couple of weeks, because her mother had been ill. She could tell the inspector that Simon had sold some of the items on ebay, and that he'd messaged her to say it was funny that two of the objects would end up in the same place, briefly, at least.

'Where would that be?' asked Inspector Hornchurch.

'Some kind of Sci-Fi Convention I think,' Bella replied. 'It's called Geek Camp, but I've never been to it. Nor has Simon, as far as I know.'

'And how well do you know Simon?'

'We're just friends. Good friends, that's all,' Bella replied.

'But you're the person he emailed in a crisis,' said the inspector. 'Any idea why?'

'Simon reckons a good friend is like gold dust,' explained Bella. 'Much more reliable than a partner, or even family. He doesn't really have any family anyway, and he knew I'd realise the message was for real, not just some silly joke.'

'And you did,' agreed Blake. 'You came straight round, even though he'd written words like killer and kidnap. He should be proud to have you as a friend. I would be.'

Bella blushed. She wasn't used to receiving compliments, and certainly not from a police inspector.

'I'm sorry,' said Blake, 'I didn't mean to embarrass you, but you obviously are a good friend to him, and the information you've given me will help us to find him, I'm sure.'

'Are you going to that Sci-Fi event to look for him?' asked Bella. 'Can you take me?'

'Definitely not,' said the inspector. 'If the killer really has kidnapped Simon, and taken him there, it's going to be difficult enough to rescue your friend and prevent anyone else getting hurt as it is. I can't be watching out for you too, and I refuse to put a young lady in danger.'

'Don't be such an old dinosaur, ' said Bella, frustrated. 'It's my help he asked for.'

'You have helped,' the inspector reassured her. 'You've saved us hours of piecing together what happened and working out where he could have been taken. That could be what saves his life.' Seeing how distressed Bella looked, he added, 'Give me your number, and I promise I'll let you know when I find him, alright?'

Numbers exchanged; the inspector moved away to make some calls. He began to arrange a team to go with him to Geek Camp, and for local police support when they got there. He tried not to be offended at being called an old dinosaur. After all, policemen got insulted all the time, but he wasn't *that* old. In fact, he was young to have achieved his current rank, and he certainly didn't consider himself to be a dinosaur. Besides wasn't 'old dinosaur' tautology?

As he moved out of earshot, Bella pulled her phone back out of her pocket and googled Geek Camp.

****

Chapter Six

Ramilid was getting increasingly frustrated. Not only was he saddled with a pathetic human, for now, anyway; but people kept stopping him to admire his 'cosplay', ask what character he was portraying and question him about how he'd made his wings. None of which was helping him find the missing wreath. He'd expected Simon to be more help, but the useless creature was glazing over again. It was probably a combination of shock and exhaustion, but Ramilid didn't care about any of that. He needed his prisoner alert to identify the artefact he'd sold.

People were asking if they could take photos too, never realising that they were taking pictures of a real dark elf. They might have felt differently if they had.

They slipped into the Moon Base venue, just as Pop-Up Puppets started their first performance of the weekend. While Ramilid was pleased to be out of the bright sunlight, which he found uncomfortable, he was annoyed to see just how packed the room was. Pop-Up Puppets were one of the most popular performance teams at the event, and always attracted a crowd. Ramilid could just spot two of the people he'd been watching earlier, over to one side. A girl in a lab coat, with a long scarf and glasses, and somebody in a pepper pot shaped object, which at that moment had its domed lid flipped back so the occupant could watch the show. The dark elf cursed. He wasn't interested in those two. He was looking for the wreath.

Simon started to gaze around the room searching for people wearing crowns, but his eyes were drawn back to the puppet company. The set was a striped booth, reminiscent of an old fashioned Punch and Judy show, and the puppets at first glance seemed simple, with wide mouths and round heads, but the puppeteers were very clever, and had created a twenty minute spoof of Back to the Future, a well-known sci-fi film. Extra pieces of scenery were added to the booth as

35

the story progressed, and the witty way they told the tale had everybody laughing and cheering by the end of the performance. Simon didn't know whether he'd concentrated on the show because it was brilliant, or because it gave him a few minutes to focus on something other than the horror he was experiencing in real life. Perhaps both.

Now he could feel Ramilid's fingers digging into his arm again, silently urging him to keep searching. The trouble was Simon didn't know if he even wanted to identify the wreath. Wouldn't he just be making the owner a target of the terrible creature standing beside him? On the other hand, if he didn't find the object, he'd be dead anyway. In fact, Simon couldn't see any way of coming out of this alive. He just didn't want anybody else to die with him. He allowed himself, briefly, to think about Maureen, and Eddy. He'd known both of them for years and spent hours in their company, sometimes out in the countryside with their metal detectors, and on other occasions having a few drinks in the pub afterwards, whether to celebrate, or commiserate with each other. Eddy was a bit of a loner. Matey enough, and good company, but he lived alone and always talked about not wanting to be tied down or have anyone depend on him.

Maureen though, she'd been a bit like a mum to Simon, or at least that's what it felt like to him, as he didn't have an actual mother to compare her to. Older than him and Eddy, she'd had to put up with a lot of flak from the other detectorists in the early days. It had been seen as a bit of a blokey hobby, and lots of people didn't want a woman around. She'd stuck it out though, and eventually teamed up with Eddy and then Simon to form a small detectorist team. She'd taken Simon under her wing when she realised that he was a bit lonely - encouraged him to go out and mix with people sometimes, even if his shyness made that difficult. She'd been really pleased when he'd become friends with Bella, who she sometimes compared to her own grown-up daughter.

Simon began to sob openly, as he thought about Maureen's family learning that she was dead. And what about Bella? Had she read his message? He hoped now that she hadn't. He'd hate to think of her turning up at his house and finding Maureen and Eddy like that.

Ramilid was trying to drag him to the side of the space, unhappy about the attention that the sobbing man was attracting. Two young men dressed like pirates came along, one of them carrying a sword made from balloons, who stopped to ask Simon if there was anything they could do to help. They were so kind that it made him weep even more, but he was beyond speaking.

'I'll look after him,' said Ramilid curtly, dragging Simon away. The last thing he wanted was people clustering around his prisoner asking awkward questions. As soon as they were in a quiet corridor leading away from the stage Ramilid slapped him, hard.

'Concentrate,' the elf hissed. 'Find that wreath. Quickly! And if I don't think you're really trying I'll start breaking your bones. After all, you don't need fingers to spot the treasure, do you? I hope you understand what I'm saying?'

Simon nodded. He understood alright. His dark spiky hair was already standing on end. Now beads of sweat broke out on his forehead and trickled down the inside of his glasses and into his dark brown eyes. His lanky body started to shake again, with fear this time, rather than grief. He was just going to have to find the right crown, and then think of a way to save whoever was wearing it. He didn't hold out much hope.

****

Bella was sitting on the train checking her phone repeatedly, hoping for a message from Simon. Anything to tell her that he was still alive. She didn't know that his phone was lying in a pool of blood back at his house in Witney. She didn't quite know why she'd decided to make this ridiculous journey. With everything she'd told the police, they were in a much better position than she was to attempt to rescue her friend; and that's all he was – a friend. She didn't fancy him or anything. Still, the idea of him being forced to witness Maureen and

Eddy's deaths, being kidnapped and terrified, feeling alone; it distressed her so much that she couldn't just go to work and forget about it. She'd phoned her boss in the tea shop where she worked and explained that she'd had a family emergency - another one - then set off for the station.

The four and a half hours on the train felt like an eternity, and even when she got off at the station, she still had a fifteen-minute walk before she reached the holiday park where the Sci-Fi Convention was being held. Of course, she couldn't just march in without a ticket, so she bought a day pass, which turned out to be a wristband, and collected a map of the site. She could see a cluster of official looking cars in the main car park beside the entrance. She guessed they were unmarked police cars. She wondered if the inspector had found Simon yet, but thought he would have let her know if he had. He'd seemed to be a genuinely kind man.

Bella examined the map and decided that as it was the middle of the day, nearly everyone would be around the venues where all the activities were happening, rather than scattered across the caravan site. In which case that would be where Simon and the kidnapper would be too ... if they really were trying to find the objects that Simon had sold. She headed to the nearest venue where a packed audience was listening to a very entertaining interview with an actor, Adam Brown, who had played Ori, one of the dwarves in The Hobbit.

Scouring the room, she wondered if the kidnapper had thought to bring costumes to disguise themselves in. If so, it would be much harder for her to spot Simon. However, it was unlikely that this whole situation was that well planned, so she comforted herself with the thought that Simon was Simon, and she'd know him anywhere.

****

Chapter Seven

Artie was at the Book Base, looking at newly published books by some of his favourite authors, and chatting to one of them, a glamorous lady called Sam, who had long white hair tinted blue and purple at the ends where it fell around her shoulders. They were talking about the steampunk series of stories she'd recently finished writing, and Artie asked her to sign the final book in the set, which he'd just bought. She was branching out into new styles and he really wanted to try out some of her books in other genres. Now he'd seen all the books for sale, he knew he'd have to go and get some more money. There were just too many he wanted to buy, and he loved the fact that at Geek Camp, plenty of the authors were there to talk to, and to sign their books, if you wanted them to.

Further along the table Jamie was chatting to David, the author of a whole range of novelisations and factual guides, all relating to a popular sci-fi television series. The cheerful man with thick mid-brown hair and a brightly coloured shirt was smiling, delighted to be chatting about books, and his favourite programme, although occasionally he'd glance over towards his wife, the author that Artie was chatting to, with a proud smile on his face.

Emily was talking to another writer at the far end of the table, a curvy lady with light brown curls escaping from under a black top hat bedecked with steampunk goggles and with feathers stuck in the brim. Emily was buying a substantial fantasy novel which the lady was signing, joking that if Emily didn't enjoy reading it, she could always use it as a door stop. Emily laughed, knowing that she really would enjoy the book. She'd dipped into it in a couple of places and realised it was exactly her kind of read.

Artie wandered down the book table to where a large, strong looking man with short brown hair and black framed glasses was signing copies of his children's book. It was about a snail, so he had a large puppet of a snail on the table in front of him, to attract and interact with any children who came along with their parents. Getting into conversation with him, Artie learnt that this was his first launch event and he was thrilled to have the chance to take part. His enthusiasm was infectious, and Artie thought that one of the loveliest things about Geek Camp was that everyone was made welcome and their skills were celebrated.

One of the discussion panels had just finished and more people were gathering around the books, so that the family team who helped the authors to run the book table began to get rushed off their feet. Their daughter hurried off to fetch coffees for the writers and booksellers who were too busy to get away and buy their own. As she came back with the drinks, she accidently bumped into a sinister looking elf who seemed to be practically dragging an unhappy looking young man along behind him. Artie turned around just in time to see the elf turn on the girl angrily, deliberately knocking the tray of drinks out of her hands and sending coffee flying in all directions. The elf leaned over her threateningly.

'Stupid mortal!' the figure hissed, before hurrying away. The girl's parents left the book table and rushed over to see if their daughter needed help. It was so rare for all of the support team to leave the Book Base at one time that the authors looked over in concern too. The girl was alright, apart from the coffee having scalded her hand, but understandably a little upset. Geek camp was generally such a relaxed, friendly event, and no-one was ever purposefully nasty.

'Whoever that cosplayer was,' said the girl's father, through gritted teeth, 'They need to learn some manners.' The mother nodded and led the girl away to run her hand under a cold tap to ease the burning. Sam, the writer Artie had first talked to, came out from behind the table and started to help the father clear up the mess. Artie, Jamie and Emily went to help too, asking stewards to fetch cloths so they could mop up the coffee. The mess was tidied up fairly quickly, but it left everyone who had seen it feeling … unsettled. There was something about way the elf had behaved. Something dark and desperate and dangerous.

Cosplayers liked to get into character, some of the time at least, but not like that. Although things around the Book Base gradually returned to normal, everyone felt a little edgy. Still, there were books to be sold, and people who wanted to buy them.

****

Melissa and Jess had wandered along to an interview with one of the girls' favourite authors, and Alec had tagged along because – well, because Jess was interested in the session.

The interview was conducted by a trim looking man with dark hair and a neatly clipped beard. He went by the name of Dr Squee and was a popular sci-fi podcaster and radio host. He was asking the author, Robert Harkess, who was a Geek Camp regular, about his books, and Alec found he rather enjoyed listening to the gentleman's replies.

He wrote novels in the steampunk genre and was gaining increasing recognition for his work. He was a big, bearded fellow in a waistcoat and top hat, speaking of the fantastical Victorian industrial steam powered settings he created for his books. Alec was intrigued enough to decide to buy one and discover the genre for himself. Plus - perhaps if he read some of the same books as Jess, she'd notice him a bit more. He groaned. Who was he kidding? Still, no harm in buying a book, was there?

****

Mike and Lee had headed over to the space where tabletop games were set out, so that people could try out games they'd heard about but had never had the chance to play. They'd claimed they wouldn't be gone long, but their friends didn't expect to see them again for hours.

Ramilid and Simon peered into the room, but the young man denied that any of the gamers in there were wearing a crown like the one he'd sold. The elf dragged him back outside and along a narrow walkway into a garden area, then grabbed his left hand, twisting the young man's little finger back until it snapped. Simon howled with pain, but the pair were sufficiently far away from the main areas of activity that nobody heard.

'One down, nine to go,' whispered the dark elf. 'If you want that to continue to be the case, I suggest that you take this search seriously.'

****

Chapter Eight

Katy was browsing around the traders' stalls. There was so much to tempt her, from collectable sci-fi figures to steampunk jewellery and accessories. She loved the stunning bags and masks and decorative walking sticks sold by a skilled leatherworker who often came to the event. She always made sure she saved up extra money for Geek Camp, so she could do a little shopping, and like most people there, after browsing for a while, she wished she'd brought more cash with her.

She turned a corner and found a photographer offering to take photos against a greenscreen, with lots of geeky backgrounds to choose from for the finished prints. There was a couple posing for photos, a buxom girl with long brown hair and a broad smile, wearing a gorgeous Tardis dress, and a man in his late thirties, clean-shaven, with light brown hair, and an open face. He was dressed in a white shirt with dark blue trousers, topped with a colourful waistcoat with a Gallifreyan design and a bow tie. From what they were saying to the photographer, these were their wedding outfits from the year before and they were keen to get some images with Whovian backgrounds. Since that was their reason for getting the photographs, the photographer, a small bearded man with short dark hair, glasses and a slight limp, kindly offered to print up their photos against several different Dr Who backgrounds instead of just one, for the same price. Katy decided that she ought to go and find Luke. They definitely needed to get some greenscreen photos taken while they were in their Osborne and Dalek cosplays.

****

In another part of the complex Artie and Luke were at a prop making session, led by a team of professional prop builders. Luke was hoping to improve his own skills for use in building more elaborate cosplays for future events, while Artie was seriously thinking about setting up a side-line in creating and selling props and accessories. They were both too busy concentrating on the session to notice that they and the other people in the room were being watched.

'What about that one?' hissed Ramilid, pointing to a golden crown which formed a triangular point above the forehead of a girl in a long pink gown, cosplaying as Princess Aurora, who was examining some of the props on display. Simon shook his head.

'It was nothing like that. It was more – delicate looking.'

'Are you sure? If you don't identify the wreath soon, you know I'll break another of your fingers.' Simon nodded miserably, and the pair moved away to search another part of the site. The difficulty was, there were hundreds of people, most of them in Cosplay, all moving from one session to another all over the complex. By the time the two of them had searched the whole site everyone had moved around, and they had to start again. Despite the threats that Ramilid was using Simon was finding it hard to focus. The shock of what had happened, and the pain from his hand were affecting his concentration. Which he knew was likely to lead to even more pain.

****

The inspector and his team were spreading out across the complex, trying to look unobtrusive. To be honest, that was harder than he'd expected when he'd first arrived. He'd asked the team running the event if anything unusual or abnormal had happened, and they'd answered by pointing over to the crowds of aliens, robots, fantasy and anime characters milling around.

'Define normal?' replied the young woman with a grin, slipping the entry wristbands onto each of the police officers. Now they were wandering around the site feeling rather ridiculous. It was amazing how out of place a bunch of men in black or dark blue suits seemed to be at an event like this, and they were getting some rather strange looks.

The local police had supplied him with two of their men, and Blake had brought four of his own. His sergeant, Josh Riley, and three plainclothes constables Scott Baker, Henry Telford and Stan Waters. The trouble was he'd asked all of them to dress formally. To him the word convention suggested businessmen in suits, so that was what he'd asked his officers to wear for this assignment. Now he realised that he should have focused on the Sci-Fi aspect instead, or at least asked them to dress casually. He'd really wanted them all to be inconspicuous so as not to alert the kidnapper that they were onto him. No chance of that now.

With a double murder and a kidnapping Blake had expected his chief inspector to run the case, but his superior was tied up with another major situation, so Blake was still in charge of the investigation, which at the moment left him feeling slightly overwhelmed. The police aspect of it was fine, it was the fact he was trying to track down a killer at an event that was so completely outside his comfort zone that troubled him.

'Inspector?' whispered a voice close behind him. 'If you want to blend in, you'll need these.'

Bella was standing at his shoulder, clutching several pairs of sunglasses, bought from the little shop on site.

'Sunglasses?' said the inspector, surprised. 'It's not even sunny. And what are you doing here?'

'Same as you,' she replied. 'I'm trying to find Simon. Trust me about the sunglasses. If you all wear them, you can walk around as 'Men in Black' from the film? You'll look perfectly normal here and attract much less attention.'

The inspector sighed, and handed the glasses round to his officers, taking a pair for himself. A couple of them, Scott and Josh, from Blake's own team, got the reference, and even began to strut a little as they walked around. Soon other cosplayers were coming up to congratulate them and ask to take group photos. Bella couldn't help but smile, briefly. She suspected that for some of the policemen, plainclothes work had never been such fun before.

'Have you seen Simon?' the inspector asked Bella. She shook her head.

'If I had, do you think I'd be standing here calmly handing out sunglasses? I'm really scared for him.'

'I know,' replied the inspector. 'We will find him.'

He was trying to sound more positive than he actually felt. There was no guarantee that they'd guessed right; that the kidnapper had brought Simon here to locate the items he'd sold. Even if they were correct, the place was heaving with people, and it wouldn't be easy to spot the pair they were looking for.

'If you do see your friend before we do, *don't* try to approach him, alright?' said the inspector. 'Come and find me, or one of my team.' Bella nodded. She really didn't want to make things any worse for Simon than they already were.

'How did you get here, by the way?' Blake asked as they walked through the site.

'I caught the train.' Bella replied. Then she began to look embarrassed, 'Thing is, I only had enough money for a one-way ticket.'

'Fine,' said the inspector, feeling guilty. 'I'll give you a lift back, when we've found your friend; and Bella – thanks for the sunglasses. They're a great idea.'

****

Chapter Nine

Jamie and Emily had wondered off to get a cup of coffee before the next session, having first signed up for the Cosplay Competition which would take place the next day.

'Why won't you tell me what cosplay you're going to wear tomorrow?' demanded Emily.

'Because I'd rather keep you guessing,' Jamie replied with a grin. 'I've spent months working on it and I want to keep the full impact of it until tomorrow. Not that I'll get through to the final round, but it's the first time I've really gone full out with a Cosplay and I want it to be a surprise.'

'I like your Bilbo cosplay,' said Emily with an encouraging grin. 'Bilbo's always been one of my favourite characters.' Jamie just smiled. He'd chosen Bilbo precisely because he knew Emily would like it, but he didn't want to sound soft by admitting that to her.

'Where did you get The Arkenstone? It looks fantastic!' she added.

'Ebay,' he admitted. 'I couldn't resist. It has such a beautiful glow to it somehow. I've no idea what it's made of though.' Jamie unclipped the little cage that Artie had made for him, and took out the stone, passing it over to Emily. 'What do you think?'

'Some kind of semi-precious mineral?' she replied. 'It felt cool when you handed it to me, but it seems surprisingly warm now. Oddly reassuring, as if so long as you have the stone with you, all's well with the world.' She handed it back to him.

'That's how I feel about you,' said Jamie, taking it from her. 'As if....' He stopped midsentence, and blushed. Where had that come from? It was how he felt, of course, but he certainly hadn't intended to say it; and yet, when he touched the stone, the words had just – popped out.

Thankfully Emily wasn't looking scornful or embarrassed. Perhaps she hadn't heard him. Then she smiled at him and he realised that she had heard, but she didn't seem to mind. Unsure where to take the conversation Jamie stared at the stone in his hand. It looked as if it was covered in little scratches, but when he peered more closely, it appeared to be writing of some kind, although it wasn't in any language he could read. He passed it back to Emily.

'Have a look, do they seem like words to you?' Emily reach out to take the stone again, and her fingers brushed against his. For a moment it felt as if electricity was passing between them, then the feeling faded, and Emily concentrated on inspecting the stone.

'More like runes than normal writing,' she agreed, 'But there's definitely something there. Here, you'd better keep it safe; it might turn out to be valuable.' Jamie tucked the stone back into its cage and two of them stood up to head to the next item in the programme that they both fancied – a film screening. This time when their hands brushed against each other as they left the coffee shop, there was no electrical tingle, but still Emily tucked her hand into Jamie's, and they strolled to the on-site cinema hand in hand.

****

By the evening Simon had a second broken finger, though at least it was on the same hand as the first, not that he cared anymore. He wasn't expecting to survive the night, and he just wanted the pain and fear to be over. He and Ramilid were standing in a queue to go into the Star Base, and the elf's supposed cosplay was receiving a lot of admiring glances. One of the official photographers for the event, a long-haired man with a beard just starting to turn grey, and a gentle manner, came up and asked if Ramilid would pose for a photograph. Reluctantly the elf agreed, and Simon hoped the creature would be distracted for long enough that he could escape, but when Ramilid let go of his arm to strike a menacing pose, Simon found that whatever force had held him in place the night before, when his friends were killed, was pinning him in position again. There was no escape. The photographer showed the digital image to the dark elf. It was a stunning shot. Not, of course, that Ramilid was bothered about such things, but it amused him to think how the human would react if he knew that the image, he'd captured wasn't a person in a costume, but a representative of the Unseelie Court.

When the elf and his captive reached the door to go into the Star Base, they both had to hold out their arms to show their wristbands. Not that they had them, but the steward on the door nodded them through anyway. Simon gave Ramilid a puzzled look. This had been happening all day as they moved between the different venues on the site.

'It's called glamour,' said Ramilid in a disinterested fashion, as they glanced around the room. 'Making something appear to be there, when it isn't, or altering the appearance of that which is there. It's one of the gifts of my people.'

Up ahead of them, another of the official photographers, an energetic young woman with shoulder length brown hair, and a wide smile, was encouraging a group of cosplayers to pose as their Lord of the Rings themed characters. As she worked the photographer was chatting away, asking them what had inspired their cosplay choice, and which items had been handmade, to try and get them to relax into creating some eye-catching poses. She even got a cosplayer who had been clutching her cloak closed to relax enough to let the photographer take a fantastic photo of the dress the young woman had created, and to pose with her friends for a brilliant group picture. The photographer had just got a new camera and was loving the opportunity to really explore its possibilities by taking interesting shots.

Simon froze. Two of them, the ones attired as Galadriel and Elrond, were wearing wreathlike crowns. The designs were very similar, and both looked much like the one he'd sold on-line, though he wasn't sure which of the two it was. He tried to relax, hoping that Ramilid didn't feel the tension in him, and realise that he'd spotted the wreath they'd been searching for all day, but it was too late. Ramilid's eyes followed Simon's gaze and identified the wreaths.

'Which one?' the elf asked. 'Which of those is the one you sold?'

'I don't know,' whispered Simon. 'I honestly don't know. It could be either of them. They both look like silver, elfin crowns to me. I didn't pay that much attention. Maureen took the pictures, I just posted them on-line and set up the auction.'

'No matter,' said Ramilid. 'I'll retrieve both crowns.'

'Don't hurt them,' begged Simon. 'Please, don't hurt them.'

Ramilid raised one eyebrow. 'I do not take instruction from you. I will do what I need to do to recover the property of the Unseelie Court.'

The group of cosplayers, their photos taken, were moving away into the crowd, trying to get into a good position to watch the evening's performances. They strolled past several of the entertainment team, some of whom were stilt-walking, dressed in closefitting steampunk outfits, while the man who ran the team, who was trim and bearded with close-cropped greying hair and smiling eyes, kept an eye on them to make sure they no-one was about to bash into his performers and knock them off balance. Besides, he and the team did a lot of preparation for the event, and he enjoyed seeing the attendees appreciate it, so it was pleasant to mingle with the guests for a while before heading backstage to oversee the evening activities.

The Host, attired as The Joker, complete with green hair, and eye-catching make-up, was already up on the stage welcoming the audience, and announcing that the first set would be performed by a band called Jollyboat. Ramilid drew Simon back into the shadows, keeping his eyes fixed on Melissa and Alec, and the silver wreaths that they were wearing.

Melissa was leaning against Mike, and they did look like a perfect couple. To be fair, even when they weren't dressed as Galadriel and Legolas, they looked great together. Underneath her long silvery wig,

Mel's own hair was auburn, and cut into a stylish bob. She was elegantly thin, and always beautifully turned out. Mike, who was good looking himself, with blond hair and a toned body, loved being seen out with her. It wasn't just that they made an eye-catching pair. They got on well and shared a lot of interests in common. More than that, Mike knew that although Mel could be a bit bossy and annoying, always designating herself the leader of the group, and trying to have the last word, she had a kind heart too.

When Mike's grandmother had died the year before, it was Melissa who'd sat with him while he struggled to come to terms with the loss, who'd cancelled a girly spa break to go with him to the funeral, and who'd allowed him time to grieve before eventually persuading him to get his life back on track. He sometimes wished the rest of their friends could see that kinder aspect of her, but in some ways he felt honoured that he was the only one aware of her softer side. Lee came back from the bar with a tray full of drinks for the group, grumbling that it was really hard to get served as a dwarf. All the people in massive cosplays tended to get served first because frankly, they took up a lot of space at the bar, and the bar staff couldn't miss them.

Jollyboat, which was made up of two brothers, the pirates that had tried to help Simon earlier, began their set with one of them playing guitar, and the other brandishing the sword made out of balloons. Their songs were pirate themed, witty and geeky and full of puns. The audience loved them, whether they'd managed to get a seat, or were propping up the bar at the back.

The Host, who'd been introducing acts and interviews and jollying everyone along since the beginning of the event, was at the bar himself having a much-needed beer. He intended to have several more as the evening wore on, at least as soon as he'd finished introducing the final acts of the evening. He'd try to remind himself that he'd need to be up early the next morning, to introduce the preliminary round of the Cosplay Competition, but the chances were he'd forget his good intentions later on – he always did.

Chapter Ten

Jollyboat left the stage to enthusiastic applause, and Blues Harvest began to set up their equipment. There was a cheer when the band was announced, and then a general scattering of the audience as the Host requested everyone to do the 'chair conga' and move their seats to the side of the auditorium to make room for people to dance. Alec and Jess headed to the bar to buy drinks.

'I'm looking forward to Blues Harvest' said Jess. 'I'm not sure I'm up to staying on for the acts after them though. I get really tired standing up for too long.' She looked a little embarrassed. She never knew how people would take it when she admitted she had health issues. That was the trouble with an invisible disability. If you looked ok, everyone assumed you *were* ok, and some people really didn't understand if you weren't. She truly hoped Alec wasn't one of those people. If she was honest with herself, she had a bit of a soft spot for him, although she knew he was several years older than her, and probably wouldn't be interested in someone her age. If she was brave, perhaps she'd say something one day, but Jess wasn't very brave, and couldn't face trying to ask Alec out, when she couldn't imagine that he might like her back.

She only knew Alec through Melissa, who she worked with in a big public relations firm, and a random comment about a fantasy film had led to her being included in the group going to Geek Camp. Since then, the two girls had become good friends, both at work and socially. This was only Jess's third year of attending the event, but although she loved the idea of cosplay, and had enjoyed creating the character, this year she felt she didn't have the nerve to carry it off.

Mellissa's boyfriend was Mike, and he knew Lee through the gym where he worked out, but she wasn't quite sure where Alec fitted in. She finally decided that she could ask him that question, even if she never had the courage to ask him out. It was a bit embarrassing after all this time. She felt as if she should know the answer already, but sometimes she wasn't well enough to join the others on the group's occasional nights out, and Geek Camp was all about Sci-Fi, so there were gaps in her knowledge when it came to her friends' real lives.

'What got you involved in the group?' she asked Alec as they queued for the bar.

'I work with Mike, at IT-Tech,' he replied. 'He encouraged me to come long, and that's how I got to know the rest of you.' He grinned at Jess. 'To be honest, I wasn't sure it was my kind of thing, that first year, but it's grown on me. I love the atmosphere – and the company!' She smiled back, hoping he meant her company, but she wasn't really sure. Finally getting served, Alec passed her a drink, but that left her with only one hand to hold her cloak closed. Alec had noticed she'd worn it like that for most of the day.

'What's wrong?' he finally asked. 'Some kind of wardrobe malfunction? It can't be comfortable holding your cloak like that all the time.'

'It's not,' Jess agreed, 'But look – I cut it far too low.' She let the fabric fall open and Alec tried politely not to stare at her chest. He thought the cut of her dress looked lovely, and wasn't too low at all, but she was obviously embarrassed by it, and he hated seeing her look so awkward.

'Here,' he said getting out a lacy squire from one of his pockets. 'Would this help? I thought it would be a nice touch if Elrond had a handkerchief, but I don't *need* it. I've got safety pins too, if you want to pin it across the bottom of the neckline. I'm sure some period dresses had that kind of panel.' Jess could have kissed him. Well, obviously she could, seeing how she felt about him, but especially for being so understanding and not just laughing at her for how she was feeling. She knew some cosplayers could carry off quite revealing costumes and be totally comfortable with it. She thought they looked terrific. She just didn't have the body confidence to do it herself.

'It won't look quite like Arwen's dress though,' she protested.

'Does it matter? If it makes you more comfortable?' Alec replied. 'This is supposed to be fun, and if you're feeling self-conscious, you're not having fun. Besides, no one will notice.' They both knew that Melissa would notice but decided not to mention it.

She hurried off to the ladies to pin the cloth to the inside of the neckline of her dress, and came back to find Alec had somehow arranged for them to sit and watch the band from one of the raised areas at the side of the auditorium. So, he *had* heard her comment about getting tired, and done something to help. He really was one of the sweetest people she knew.

Blues Harvest came out on stage and began their set. They were a nerd-rock five-piece band who played music from the audience's favourite films and television shows and adapted the lyrics of well-known songs to fit the theme of the event. They were a popular feature of Geek Camp and as soon as they started playing music from Star Wars, most people hit the dance floor.

As many of the dancers were wearing cosplay, it was an amazing sight. Stormtroopers were bopping away with Discworld characters, and a Groot was dancing, albeit stiffly, with a rather clumsy ET. To be fair, those were tricky cosplays to dance in. A visually impaired man in a Micky Mouse cosplay, using his white stick to judge the space around him, was dancing beside an impressive Uruk-Hai Orc, and another man who was cosplaying as the Second Doctor was prancing happily in and out between the other dancers, while pretending to play his blue and white striped recorder.

A woman cosplaying as a handmaid from A Handmaid's Tale, was dancing with a man who was Princess Leia from Star Wars, wearing a full length white dress and with his own long dark hair pinned up in buns on each side of his head, a look he carried off rather well. Jess watched the dancers slightly wistfully as she wondered how the handmaid could see where she was moving with such a big bonnet obscuring her view.

'Would you rather be dancing?' asked Alec softly. 'You don't have to sit here with me if you'd rather not.'

'I *want* to be here with you,' Jess replied, perhaps a little too emphatically. 'It would be lovely to have the energy to dance, but I don't, and sitting down means that I can stay for the whole set, which is great; but if you want to dance, I don't want to stop you.'

'I'm fine here. Happy to sit and enjoy the set – with you.'

As they watched the concert, Artie, who was walking back from the bar, noticed that Alec and Jess, who he'd met that morning, were being watched by the decidedly creepy dark elf he'd seen earlier threatening the girl from the Book Base. The figure was still holding onto the arm of the tired, stressed looking young man in a grubby t-shirt, who was now holding his left hand awkwardly. Artie was pretty sure they weren't part of the same group, and there was something sinister about the way they were looking at just those two members of the audience, rather than the band. He headed back to where the rest of his friends were standing but kept glancing over at the dark elf. He was sure something was wrong, but he couldn't exactly explain what, so he didn't mention it to the others. Katy and Luke were attempting to dance, but once again, Luke was discovering the limitations of being a Dalek.

Jamie and Emily were killing themselves laughing at their friends' efforts on the dance floor, and Artie couldn't help but notice that the two of them seemed closer somehow. He wondered if Jamie had finally found the courage to say something to Emily about how he felt about her. He'd told Artie often enough, which was tricky really, because if Jamie was gay, Artie would have asked him out in a heartbeat, but he'd always known that was never going to happen. Jamie was straight, and in love with Emily, and that was just how things were. He was even happy for them both, although at that moment the happiness was tinged with just a trace of sadness.

Blues Harvest finished their set with a Ghostbusters number, and there was another short break as the next entertainment set up.

'Do you want to head back to the caravan now?' Alec asked Jess. 'I'll walk you back if you like.'

'I don't need walking back,' Jess replied. 'And I don't want to drag you away.'

'You wouldn't be dragging me,' Alec admitted. 'I'm tired. I've had a really stressful week at work and I'm feeling a bit burnt out. I'm happy to go back if you don't mind the company?'

They wriggled their way through the crowd to find Mel, Mike and Lee, and tell them that they were heading back. The others opted to stay on at the venue a bit longer, to listen to Leroy, the DJ who was on next, so Alec and Jess left alone.

Artie happened to glance up just as they were leaving and noticed that the dark elf and the young man with him followed them out. He was sure something was wrong, but he didn't know what to do about it. He slipped away from his friends and began to follow the followers.

****

Chapter Eleven

Inspector Blake Hornchurch was becoming increasingly frustrated. The tech team back at the crime scene had gone through Simon's emails and identified the buyer of the stone as Jamie Patterson. Enquiries on the site had told them which caravan he and his friends were staying in, but nobody had been back there all day. Trying to stay incognito, so as not to alert the kidnapper and put Simon's life at increased risk, meant they couldn't just post a policeman outside the van or stick a sign on it. In the end Blake had decided to write Jamie a note asking him to call the inspector's number immediately and shoved it under the door.

The team hadn't had any luck identifying the purchaser of the second object, though they had found a photo of the crown Simon had sold. That left them searching for Simon, anyone wearing that type of crown, and someone carrying a stone, amongst a couple of thousand people all milling around and wearing very distracting cosplays. It was one of the most bizarre days he could remember in a long career in the police.

As a murder hunt, it was very contained. As far as he could tell, everyone the police had any interest in was on site in the holiday park. He wished he could just put out a public announcement to everyone, asking certain people to contact him, or warn other people that a dangerous criminal was amongst them, but as well as causing panic that would probably get Simon killed.

He'd positioned his own officers in the two venues where the various evening activities were being held, while he and the two local members of his team moved around between them. He had to remind the junior officers that they were there to observe, not to enjoy the music, but he couldn't blame them. The whole event had a kind of quirky, good natured charm that sucked you in, even if you weren't into sci-fi or fantasy. When he went to speak to his officers in the

COLD DEAD COSPLAY

Moon Base, he found them watching a man wearing an Edwardian looking explorer's outfit with a Union Jack waistcoat and a pith helmet, whose performance involved an unusual blend of hip-hop and comedy, with a steampunk vibe. He was called Professor Elemental, and the crowd loved him; even Blake's police officers, Josh and Scott, were laughing.

The next time the inspector looked into that venue there was a prog rock band called Hats off Gentlemen It's Adequate playing scientific and sci-fi themed songs, or so his sergeant explained. The inspector decided that he had no idea what prog rock meant, though he could pick out a little strand of contemporary classical music in there, along with some metal and funk. He liked some of the lyrics but couldn't imagine listening to it at home, though he found he did begin to enjoy it as a live gig. He felt old. Then he noticed that some of the audience who were obviously appreciating the band's music were undoubtedly older than him, so maybe it wasn't an age thing. Perhaps he was just boring. He couldn't decide which was worse, especially as Bella's 'old dinosaur' comment was still niggling away at him.

He noticed Josh disappear off to the side of the space and come back clutching a copy of the band's CD. He felt he ought to remind them again that they were there to work, but he knew his team well enough to realise that they were paying attention to the audience, even if it didn't look like it, and if they spotted anything important, they'd act on it immediately. In the meantime, he supposed it didn't matter if they enjoyed themselves while they were working. He wondered whether Henry and Stan were having as much fun in the other venue.

He worried about where Bella had got to, and hoped she was safe. He was concerned that if she spotted her friend, she'd be tempted to charge in to help him, and put herself at risk. Not that she was his responsibility, exactly. She'd chosen to come looking for Simon, but Blake couldn't help worrying about her.

He also admitted to himself that she'd been very helpful, not just in assisting them to piece together what might have happened to Simon, but also with her Men in Black suggestion. It had made their investigation rather more subtle, though it had also brought home to him that he did have an old-fashioned tendency to choose male officers for a lot of what he thought of as the riskier aspects of police work.

Many of the female cosplayers were dressed as powerful women characters, and he found it quite thought provoking. He'd never thought of himself as sexist, and had certainly supported and put forward a number of his female officers for promotion in the past; but brought face to face with the fact that he hadn't picked a single female officer to join him on this investigation, he realised that perhaps he needed to review his thinking, although first he needed to catch a killer.

****

Bella was moving between the two entertainment venues, but getting increasingly frustrated, mainly by her own height. She wasn't tall enough to see over the heads of other audience members and was worried that Simon could be just meters away from her and she wouldn't be able to spot him. She was terrified that the kidnapper would kill her best friend. She'd only known him for a couple of years, but they got on really well. They'd even talked about dating, at one point, but decided they didn't really fancy each other in that way and valued their friendship too much to risk messing it up. Not dating, they'd agreed, meant that they could be friends for life, though at the moment she was worried about exactly how long that might be, in Simon's case.

She was standing between the two venues when she saw a couple of Lord of the Rings cosplayers walk out of the Star Base. They were followed by a dark, elven looking creature, who seemed to be dragging somebody along with him. Because he was on the far side of the elf to Bella, she couldn't be sure it was Simon, but it might be. Behind them another young man in jeans and t-shirt was trying to follow inconspicuously. Bella was torn. Should she follow all of them and confirm that it really was Simon, or go and fetch the inspector? In the end she took note of the direction everyone was heading in, then dived into the Moon Base to fetch the police.

****

Alec and Jess were walking along a dimly lit path which lead to the part of the site where they and the rest of their friends were staying. They'd booked a large caravan that could sleep six, though caravan was hardly a fair description. That made it sound small and cramped, whereas this place was fairly roomy, it had central heating and was well equipped. There were three separate bedrooms, and two bathrooms, and they were all feeling smug about how great their accommodation was.

Jess couldn't wait to get back and put the kettle on. Alcohol was great, but sometimes you just needed a coffee, and a chance to sit down and relax; especially with someone you rather liked. They were walking slowly, as Jess was becoming really tired, and chatting to each other, so they didn't notice the sound of someone following them, and softly circling round to get ahead.

Suddenly they were confronted by a strange figure dressed as an elf, standing on the path directly in front of them. Beside him was a second man with a scratched face, wearing jeans and a t-shirt, and looking terribly distressed, who tried to lunge towards them, as if to get between them and the dark elf.

'Run!' the man cried, before seeming to freeze in his tracks. An unpleasant smile crossed the face of the menacing figure in front of them. He reached out a hand and the crown flew off Alec's head and landed in it. Clasping it tightly, the elf tried to sense if it had any latent power; he didn't think so, but that didn't mean it definitely wasn't the item he was searching for.

'What are you doing?' Alec protested. 'You can't take that. It's mine!' He reached forward to retrieve the crown and Ramilid made a slashing motion at him. Even though the creature didn't appear to touch him, gashes appeared in Alec's chest, showing through rips in his robe, and blood spurted from his rib cage. Jess screamed, then pulled her cloak off and flung it at the elf before kneeling down beside Alec.

Even as she tossed the cloak Jess realised it was a mistake. How was a lump of fabric supposed to stop someone so violent? It didn't. Angered at Jess's effrontery Ramilid tossed the cloak to the ground and reached towards her. At that moment Artie flung himself at the dark elf from the side, and Simon, freed from whatever force had frozen him while the elf was distracted, fell forward and landed on Alec.

Simon was torn between running from the fight; taking his first opportunity to escape after twenty-four hours of hell or trying to protect the others from the danger he'd brought on them. He'd never thought of himself as a brave man, but somehow, he found the courage to turn and face his tormentor.

Ramilid had thrown Artie to the ground and was using some enchantment to raise plant tendrils up through the earth to wrap around the young man's arms and legs to pin him there. The elf closed his fist tightly and to Artie it felt as if something was gripping his heart, squeezing it until it felt as if it was going to burst inside his body. Jess and Simon charged at Ramilid at the same time, both yelling at him to leave the young man alone.

By this time the noise of the attack had drawn the attention of the inspector who, together with Josh and Scott, had been alerted by Bella. They came charging along the path towards the group, followed by Bella herself, who'd decided her best chance of finding Simon was to follow the police team. They all had a brief glimpse of a dark figure as it flung two people to the ground without even seeming to lay a hand on them, and then vanished. The inspector couldn't be completely sure that the thing hadn't simply stepped into the shadows, but he had a nasty feeling it had actually dematerialised before his eyes. He glanced at his team and saw that they looked shocked too. They had all seen the kidnapper just - disappear.

Chapter Twelve

Jess had picked up her cloak and was trying to use it to stop Alec's blood from pumping out of his chest. Josh went to assist her, but even with two of them attempting to stem the bleeding, it didn't seem to be helping. The inspector phoned for a couple of ambulances, although looking at Alec's slashed chest he wasn't sure help would arrive in time.

His constable, Scott, was kneeling next to Artie, using a Swiss Army Knife to cut through each of the roots that were holding the young man to the ground. It wasn't exactly a standard police issue gadget, but it was a surprisingly useful tool in a crisis. Blake decided he might get one for himself.

Bella had her arms around Simon, who was slumped on the ground shaking. Now that Ramilid was gone, the young man couldn't hold it together anymore. The inspector could see that it was far too soon to try to take a statement, but there were a few things he had to know at once. He crouched down beside Simon and wondered how to phrase his questions.

'Did that thing get what it wanted? Is it still going after anyone? What are we dealing with? Can you tell me?'

'He's a dark elf,' Simon's voice was a rasping whisper. 'Called Ramilid. He took the crown, not sure it's the right one though. This group had two similar ones. Wants stone too, from caravan...caravan...' he was struggling to remember.

'We know the number,' the inspector spoke reassuringly. He could see the young man had broken bones, was in a lot of pain, and suffering from shock. Surely that would explain the dark elf comment, wouldn't it? But then again, they'd all seen the creature vanish, and what normal person could tie somebody to the ground by making roots grow up through the soil?

****

Ramilid was crouched on top of a nearby caravan, looking down on the action. He saw an ambulance crew arrive and begin to treat the man whose crown he'd taken, while a policeman freed the young man who'd leapt on him from the tendrils he'd been trapped by. Of course, even from here, Ramilid could use his powers to crush the young man's heart again and finish him off, but in fairness, he had no real grudge against him. He'd just leapt to someone's defence, as any friend might do.

Besides, the elf knew he'd be better off not drawing any more attention to himself, not while the police were around, and not until he'd retrieved the other crown, and the stone. Then, and only then, would he allow himself the luxury of killing Simon. Just because his prisoner had escaped him for the moment, that didn't mean that he didn't deserve to be punished for stealing the Hoard. For now, Ramilid decided to keep out of sight and try to get hold of the other objects. He no longer needed Simon for that.

****

Alec was still alive, but had lost a lot of blood, and the paramedics were trying not to get peoples' hopes up. Jess was a little bruised from being thrown to the ground, but otherwise unhurt, although all her joints were aching. She insisted on going in the first ambulance with Alec, and the inspector took her name and number, checked which caravan she and her friends were staying in and arranged to speak to her later. He sent one of the local police officers to the hospital too, to protect them, just in case the attacker decided to follow them there.

Artie was very shaken up, and had pains in his chest, but the paramedics didn't think he'd suffered any lasting damage. The young man refused to go to hospital while his friends might be in danger, although he agreed to get checked out the next day.

It was Simon who gave the inspector the greatest dilemma. He obviously required medical treatment, but the police needed his help. In the end it was Simon who suggested a compromise. The paramedics straightened and strapped his broken fingers, and gave him pain relief, on condition that the police agreed to take him to hospital to be x-rayed the next day and receive further treatment if he needed it. They also insisted that Simon had some food and water before doing anything else, but the inspector could see that for himself. The man had had a nightmarish twenty-four hours, and the creature hadn't allowed him anything to drink, let alone eat.

The inspector took Simon to an office on the site that the organisers had offered to the police as a base, and Simon sunk into a chair. Bella, who'd insisted on accompanying them, stood protectively beside her friend.

'You needn't look at me like that,' said the inspector. 'I'm not going to arrest him. I'm not even going to take a formal statement until tomorrow. I just need any information he can give me to stop the ... kidnapper attacking anyone else.'

'I don't think you can,' Simon answered, a little hazy from the painkillers. 'He's powerful - magic-type powerful. I know that sounds weird but it's true. He said that the things we'd dug up, Maureen and Eddy and me, were a Fairy Hoard and he'd come to retrieve them. He took back what was at my house and killed the others. He'd have killed me too, as a punishment, but he needed me to find the things we'd sold. He did kill the others, didn't he? I didn't imagine it?'

'You didn't imagine it, I'm afraid. What did he do to your friend Eddy? How was that even possible?'

'Crows,' answered Simon. 'He used crows.'

Nobody had spoken for a couple of minutes, when the door opened and Henry, another of Blake's constables, came in with a tray of food, some water and several paper cups filled with coffee. It wasn't only Simon who hadn't had time for food that day. They pulled some more office chairs up to the table and began to eat, although after the conversation they'd just had, none of them were feeling that hungry.

The inspector stared into his coffee cup, trying to remember the collective noun for crows. He had an odd feeling it was "A Murder of Crows" which now seemed far more literal than he would ever have imagined.

****

Simon was so exhausted that he fell asleep before he'd even finished eating, with his head resting on his uninjured arm on the table, between the scattered coffee cups. Bella looked at the inspector defiantly.

'Don't you dare wake him up!'

'I wasn't about to,' said Blake smiling at her. 'I imagine that sleep's the best thing for him. Are you sure you two are just friends? You're very protective of him. Where did you meet?'

'In the tea shop where I work,' Bella replied. 'It's not far from his house, and he came in with Maureen one day.' Her face clouded over. 'She really was like a mother to him.' They were both quiet for a few minutes.

'Why a tea shop?' asked Blake, to break the silence.

'Why not?' replied Bella sharply, 'It's where I work. Everybody works somewhere.'

'You just don't strike me as someone who works in a teashop,' countered Blake.

'It's a very nice tea shop! And what's it got to do with the police, anyway?' said Bella, getting huffy.

'I'm not asking as a policeman, I'm just making conversation.' Blake grinned, 'I would have thought you had the potential to do all sorts of things, so why work in a tea shop?'

'I did have other plans, when I was younger,' Bella admitted, 'But my father got ill when I was studying for my A Levels. I didn't get the grades I'd hoped for, and my family needed help, so my "career" took a different path.'

'What did you want to do?' asked Blake.

'You'll laugh if I tell you.' Bella glared at him through narrowed eyes.

'I promise I won't,' he said, 'Go on, tell me, please Bella. I genuinely want to know.'

'I had planned to apply to the police force,' said Bella, looking embarrassed. 'Seems silly now, doesn't it?'

Blake chuckled.

'You promised not to laugh,' said Bella indignantly.

'I'm not laughing at the idea of you joining the police,' Blake tried to re-assure her. 'It's just that I had a hunch that that was what you'd say. And it's not too late, you know. There are all sorts of routes in, like apprenticeships. It just takes a little longer.'

'It's too late now, anyway.'

'Hardly,' replied Blake. 'You're only...what? Twenty-one? Twenty-two?'

'Twenty-three!' she snapped.

'Ah, I see your problem,' said Blake, with a serious look on his face, 'You are indeed ancient!'

Bella laughed and flicked an empty paper cup at him, which he dodged, neatly.

'Seriously though,' she added when they'd both stopped chuckling, 'I'm not sure I could deal with what we're dealing with now, all this *strange* stuff. Not all the time.'

'Trust me,' said Blake. 'I've never dealt with anything like this in my career until now, and I don't expect to ever again. Don't let it put you off the idea of joining the force.'

****

In the hospital Jess was sitting in a corridor waiting for news. Alec had been taken up to theatre for surgery, and she was still clutching her bloodstained cloak. The dark patch on it was large enough, but she knew that most of his blood had spilled onto the ground. She didn't know if anyone could survive losing that much blood, and she wasn't sure how deep the damage had gone, whether the creature had cut through into Alec's organs. All she could do was sit there and wait until somebody came to tell her something.

She was feeling self-conscious, sitting in a modern hospital dressed as a medieval elf, but that wasn't really what was troubling her. She was wishing she'd had the nerve to tell Alec she liked him. The worst that could have happened was that he'd have kindly pointed out that she was too young, or not his type. Now she doubted she'd ever get the chance to say it, and her imagination was filled with "if onlys", which was marginally better than thinking about the creature that had attacked them, and the strange powers he'd used against them. Jess didn't feel she could even begin to process that. Not until she knew what was happening with Alec, anyway.

****

Chapter Thirteen

Artie was heading back towards the Star Base, accompanied by Scott, who admitted that he was starting to feel rather awkward. Men in Black had worked as a group cosplay, or even when they were in pairs, but not for a single policeman, especially now it was much too dark to wear sunglasses.

As they reached the Star Base a small group of people were coming out of it to cross to the Moon Base. They consisted of a tall man in a Brit-Cit Judge cosplay, from Judge Dredd, all black leather and with additional padded armour plates on his shoulders, chest and knees. His cosplay was topped off by a fierce looking helmet in black, red and gold, and for a moment Scott looked alarmed. The red-haired woman with the judge smiled at the two young men to reassure them. She wore a long shiny black coat over a red corset, black trousers and boots, and lifted her steampunk style goggles away from her eyes to see them better.

'Durham Red?' asked Artie, and the woman grinned. Turning to explain to Scott, he said 'She's a mutant vampire bounty hunter from Strontium Dog.' Scott didn't feel any the wiser, but did admire both cosplays, and the one worn by the teenage girl who was with them, who explained she was cosplaying as Vasquez from Aliens; in camouflage trousers, a black vest top and a red and white bandanna round her head, half covering her brown hair, and carrying a stylized weapon which was just on the right side of Geek Camp rules. Scott was relieved to have at least heard of the film Aliens: he was beginning to understand that Sci-Fi covered a lot more ground than he'd realised.

The man chuckled in a friendly way and wandered over to the policeman, removing his helmet to reveal neatly trimmed brown hair and beard and a broad smile.

'Feeling a bit out of place?' he asked. 'Don't worry, the first year I came to Geek Camp I was pretty formal, wore a suit for some of it, but you soon relax into it. By the next time I came along I was dressed as a jedi knight. Here, you drinking?' He offered a flask to the policeman, who had to resist the urge to reply that he was on duty. As all the police were trying to blend in, Scott accepted, but only took a small sip. Just as well, since the rum in the flask was pretty strong.

'Thanks,' said Scott, handing it back. 'I don't suppose you've seen anyone dressed as an elf, have you?'

'There are loads of elves this year,' the girl replied, as the man produced another flask out of his numerous pockets and handed it to Artie.

'You look like you could really use a drink,' he said. Artie accepted gratefully. He was certainly glad of something to settle his nerves, although finding himself drinking mead was an unexpected but pleasant surprise.

'This elf is a bit different looking,' said Scott. 'Kind of dark and brooding.'

'With dark wings,' added Artie. 'Not Tolkien style at all.'

'I think I saw him in the queue, earlier this evening,' the woman answered. 'But that was hours ago. It can get a bit stressful when you can't find your friends, can't it?'

'Hold on,' said the girl, suddenly. 'I know the one you mean; I saw him in the Star Base. Over in the far corner, beyond the bar, a few minutes ago.'

'I hope you find your friend,' said the man, as the family group moved away to go to the other venue.

'So do I,' said Scott to Artie, 'Though at least he won't be able to attack anyone in there. It's far too crowded.' The pair of them entered the Star Base and started to search. Artie was looking for his friends, though it was hard to spot them on the crowded dance floor. When he finally located them, he realised that Jamie was missing.

'Don't worry,' said Emily in reply to Artie's question about him. 'He's just nipped to the gents; he'll be back in a minute.'

Both Artie and the policeman were looking round, but couldn't see either Jamie, or the dark elf. Scott couldn't even spot Stan, his fellow officer, although he knew he had to be in there somewhere. To be honest, with the stage being the only brightly lit area in the venue, it wasn't easy to see anyone in the shadows at the edges of the room. Artie began to tingle with nerves. Surely the creature wouldn't attack Jamie there, would he?

****

Jamie was walking back from the Gent's toilets and heading for the bar. He planned to buy one last round of drinks before the night's entertainment wrapped up. With everyone focused around the dance floor and the bar area, the corridor he was walking down was empty and dimly lit. The first moment he realised that something was wrong was when the lights in the corridor flickered out completely. He could still see the soft glow of the dance floor up ahead, and strangely he noticed that the Arkenstone he was wearing seemed to be glowing too. He hadn't realised it did that, not so visibly, anyway. The next moment he saw a dark figure in front of him, reaching for his neck. Ramilid grasped the leather cord and twisted it, causing Jamie to gasp. The dark elf tried to pull at the thong, which was holding the caged stone, but it was made from new leather, and wouldn't snap easily. Jamie was trying to wrench himself free, so Ramilid reached one hand round behind the young man's head, intending to twist and snap his neck. Dead people don't struggle, and the elf wanted to retrieve the stone quickly and get out of the building before he was spotted.

The Host suddenly came stumbling along the corridor, in a hurry to get to the Gent's. His good intentions had dissolved and yet again he'd had a few too many drinks and was feeling the effects. He already knew that tomorrow was going to be hell. In the dark corridor he didn't even see Ramilid until he crashed into him, causing all three of them to land on the floor in a heap.

Suddenly he felt terrified, though he couldn't have said why. The cosplayer he had landed on felt strange – cold and frightening. The figure slid out from underneath him and leaned over the Host, until he could feel bitter breath in his face. This was no cosplayer. He was sure of it. The Host felt sick. Really sick, but this time it was due to fear, not alcohol. The person at the bottom of the heap groaned, and the creature turned his attention back to the man who was groggily trying to sit up. There were shouts coming from the far end of the corridor. Knowing that he had to escape quickly, Ramilid reached down and made a slashing gesture across Jamie's chest with his hand, cutting through the leather thong and freeing the stone in its metal cage. By the time Artie and the policeman reached them, the Host's head was spinning, Jamie was crumpled on the floor and the dark elf was gone.

****

Emily was looking around the dance floor, a worried expression on her face. The way Artie had asked where Jamie was, and then hurried off, worried her. Now she couldn't see either of them. Above a short gap in the music she heard shouting off to one side and began to weave her way towards the sound. Stan, the constable who'd been on duty in the Star Base all evening, was also hurrying in that direction, and he and Emily reached the corridor at the same time.

Emily freaked out when she saw Jamie slumped on the floor with blood oozing from his chest. Artie was kneeling beside him, looking at the wound, while Scott was calling the inspector with one hand, while shining a torch to give Artie some light with the other. Stan took the torch from his colleague and shone it directly onto Jamie so that Artie could examine him more easily.

'It's not as bad as what that thing did to Alec,' Artie said with relief, flicking his long fringe out of his eyes. 'It looks like a single cut. Not too deep, but who knows what it could get infected with.' Emily stared at him in confusion, as did the Host. Neither of them knew what he was talking about, and Artie couldn't even begin to think how to explain it.

Scott offered the Host a hand to get to his feet, but the shaken man preferred to stay on the floor. He looked really pale, even his green hair appeared a little washed out by the light of the torch.

'I think I'll stay here, thanks,' he said, with a shaky smile. 'Just until the world stops spinning.'

'I'm sorry you got caught up in this,' said Scott, 'But if it's any consolation, by crashing into the killer like that, you probably saved this young man's life.'

Somehow hearing the word "killer" didn't console the Host at all. It didn't surprise him either. The vibe that creature had given off was pure evil. Knowing it had actually killed though, that was terrifying. It could have killed him, or the 'hobbit' it had attacked or anyone. The world was spinning again, and he briefly wondered if going tee-total would make him feel better. Probably not. He scraped enough braincells together to ask a rather important question. 'Where did that thing go?'

'We have no idea!' replied the policeman.

****

Chapter Fourteen

Ramilid hadn't actually gone anywhere. He was still in the corridor watching them, but using glamour magic to mask his presence. It was difficult to maintain for long in front of multiple people though, and it was spreading his ability thin. Eventually he slipped through a door in the darkened corridor into the Ladies toilets and had to crawl ignominiously out of a window to escape.

Once outside he looked at the stone he'd cut from the young man's neck. He could sense the power in it. Enough to tempt him, briefly, to keep it for himself rather than returning it to the Unseelie Court. However, knowing how powerful his Queen was, he doubted he could get away with it. Still it was something to consider, once he'd recovered the other items, and punished those who had stolen them.

He regretted not having the chance to kill the stone carrier, but he wasn't worth going back for. Ramilid didn't want to get too distracted from his mission. He still had the other crown to retrieve, and then the silver chalice, though that would have to wait, for now. He heard the sound of sirens approaching and running footsteps heading towards the Star Base and slid away into the shadows.

****

The paramedics, surprised to be called to the same location twice, had cleaned the wound on Jamie's chest, closed it up with butterfly stitches and then applied a protective bandage. They didn't feel he needed to be admitted to hospital as the single slash on his chest wasn't too deep, though it was obviously painful, and his neck was rather sore, but otherwise he'd come off lightly. By this time Luke and Katy had caught up with them and were trying to make sense of what had happened.

The inspector asked the Host not to mention what he'd seen to anyone other than the event organisers. It would only cause panic, and that could make the creature even more dangerous. They knew who it was targeting now, so as long as they could protect those people, everyone else should be safe. The Host nodded weakly in agreement. He had no idea how he could explain what he'd seen to anyone anyway. One of the local police constables escorted him back to his accommodation and he collapsed onto his bed thankful to be alive.

****

Now Jamie was back in their caravan with Emily, Artie, Katy and Luke. The inspector was sitting opposite them, trying to explain what was going on. Not exactly a straightforward task.

'So it... he... was after the Arkenstone?' asked Jamie, 'And he would have killed me for it?'

'Arkenstone?' the inspector was puzzled.

'That's what I was using it as,' Jamie explained, 'For my cosplay, but it sounds like it was actually something else.'

'It did seem special though,' added Emily. 'And it had some runes carved into it.'

'I wish I'd taken a better look at it this morning,' said Luke. 'I don't suppose we'll see it again now.'

'I doubt it,' the inspector agreed. 'But that's not why I'm here. You need to decide what you want to do. We know that the ... creature ... is still here. We've no reason to think he'll attack you again. He's got what we believe he was after, from you, anyway, but we can't guarantee it. It might be safer for all of you to leave the site now and go home. We can give you a police escort, for safety.'

The inspector thought they'd agree immediately, grateful to get away from the place. He hadn't expected howls of protest.

'But then we'll miss the Cosplay Competition!' complained Emily.

'The Dark Room is on tomorrow night,' added Luke.

'I'd planned to get some greenscreen shots taken, with both of us in cosplay,' Katy muttered to Luke.

'You're the two who've been attacked by him.' The inspector turned to Jamie and Artie. 'What do you want to do?'

The two young men looked at each other and nodded in agreement.

'I really don't want to go home tonight,' Jamie admitted sheepishly. 'I've spent months working on my cosplay for the competition. I want to stay.'

'And I need to go back to the Book Base,' said Artie firmly. 'There are loads of books I want to buy, and if I get them here, I can chat to the authors and get them signed. We'll stick together the whole time. Go everywhere as a group and look out for each other.'

The inspector shook his head in disbelief. 'So, you're determined to stay because of books, photos, and a costume competition?'

'**Cosplay**!' they all corrected him.

'And The Dark Room,' repeated Luke.

'What's the dark room?' asked the inspector, perplexed.

The friends looked at each other and shrugged. There was no way they could explain that particular entertainment to the inspector. You either got it or you didn't, and they were pretty sure he wouldn't understand.

It was Emily who took pity on the worried man sitting in front of them.

'I know it must seem crazy, that we want to stay after what's happened, but Geek Camp – it's special to all of us. We look forward to it all year, spend months planning and building our cosplays, and enjoy spending time other people who all like the same things. It's brilliant.'

'It's like an extended family, and everyone looks forward to meeting up each year,' Jamie chipped in. 'The best thing is that people hardly ever ask you what you do for a living. Here, it doesn't matter if you work in a bar or as a barrister. If you like the same films or books or shows you all hang out together.'

'Which does make it pretty special,' added Artie, 'So we're staying. Anyway, if we went home now, we'd all be scattered. We live in different places. We'd rather be together, after everything that's happened.'

Everyone nodded and the inspector sighed, knowing he wasn't going to persuade them. All he could do was assign a couple of his team to keep a watchful eye on the group and hope they wouldn't be attacked again. Not that he was sure what his men could do if they were.

****

Chapter Fifteen

Jess was still at the hospital, waiting for news about Alec. She suddenly realised that her friends might not know where the two of them had disappeared off to, so she called Mel's mobile. The first few times Melissa didn't pick up, because there was a lot of noise as everyone left the venues at the end of the evening and headed back to their caravans. When she did answer the phone, she couldn't make any sense of what Jess was saying. Surely the two of them were just back at the van, chatting. Maybe Jess had had too much to drink and started imagining things? She wasn't much of a drinker usually, but everyone let their hair down at Geek Camp.

By this time Melissa, Mike and Lee had reached the door of their caravan and found two of the Men in Black cosplayers waiting for them. Or, as it turned out, policemen. Jess had given the inspector the caravan number before getting in the ambulance with Alec, and by now the dark elf knew the police were on site, so there was no reason why the constables, Henry and Stan, couldn't wait by the van for its occupants to come back. What they told Mel and her friends seemed incredible. So did the fact that Alec was in hospital, critically injured, but they had no choice but to believe them.

****

The inspector went to the office to fill Simon in on what had happened. The young man was relieved that Ramilid had got the stone back without killing or badly injuring anyone, but he was still frantic about whoever the dark elf might target next.

'Isn't there any way I can help?' he begged, 'It's all my fault. If we'd declared the find, taken it to the coroner like you're supposed to, that creature wouldn't have come after anyone.'

'He'd probably have gone after the coroner,' said Bella, trying to reassure her friend.

'I've got an armed response team just outside the site,' said the inspector, trying to sound reassuring, 'And everyone on my team has been issued with tasers, but I just don't know what will work against him. Nobody does,' his shoulders slumped forward, and he looked so lost that Bella felt sorry for him.

'You could try cold iron,' she said, handing the inspector her iPhone, on which she'd been googling "How to protect yourself from Fairies." 'Or salt,' she added. 'Apparently they don't like salt.'

'Somehow I think it would take more than a pinch of salt to get rid of Ramilid,' said Simon. He looked at the inspector, a puzzled frown on his face, then asked, 'Why haven't you arrested me yet?'

'Arrested you? What on earth for? You're not the one going around killing people.'

'No,' Simon agreed, 'But we didn't declare our find, and that's illegal. I really ought to be sent to prison for starting all this.'

'I think you've been punished enough already,' said the inspector firmly, 'And I've no idea how I'm going to write this case up as it is, without charging you with anything. My superiors are going to think I've gone mad.' He stood up adding, 'If you really want to help, come with me to see if you can identify the crown you sold. I'd like to know what we're dealing with, before that - elf - gets hold of this one too.' Blake glanced at Bella. 'Cold iron? Any ideas what type of iron?'

'Horseshoes,' she replied.

'How on earth do I requisition those?' groaned the inspector.

****

Melissa was huddled on the sofa in the caravan, Mike's arm wrapped round her protectively, while Lee stared at the inspector, and Simon, in horror.

'So, I need you to let Simon here look at the crown you're wearing, to see if he thinks it's the one he sold you on ebay.'

Simon's bandaged hand was more convincing than the inspector's strange explanation. That and the fact that Alec was in hospital. Slowly Mel removed the crown and passed it over. Simon turned it round and round in his hands, examining it closely.

'I don't know,' he said quietly, 'I'm sorry. It's got a certain weight to it, and it's delicate and well made, but I can't be sure if it's the one I sold or not. Your friend's crown looked similar.'

'Either way,' the inspector announced, 'It would be safer to give it to us to look after. If you haven't got it, you can't be attacked for it.'

'No!' replied Melissa. 'Why should I? Its mine isn't it!?'

'Of course it is; but it makes you a target,' Blake explained.

'Then protect me,' she argued, 'You're the police, aren't you? You're supposed to protect people. I need the crown for the Cosplay Competition. I promise you. I'll hand it over after the preliminary round in the morning, and only take it back for the evening if we get through to the Final.'

'You can't still be planning to enter the Cosplay Competition?' asked Mike. 'Not now?'

'It was supposed to be a group entry,' Lee added. 'What about Alec and Jess?'

'We'll just be a smaller group!' Melissa was determined to go ahead, whatever anyone said. Mike knew she had a stubborn streak, but he'd never seen her be so unreasonable before, and he wasn't sure what to make of it.

'Well I won't enter the competition without them,' growled Lee. As far as the inspector was concerned, that made him the sanest person in the room.

COLD DEAD COSPLAY

Lee pulled off his long wig and beard to reveal very short brown hair and a gloomy expression. He really wasn't happy about the way Melissa was reacting.

Simon couldn't believe what he was hearing, either, but then, he'd seen Ramilid in action, been held prisoner by him for twenty-four hours, and this girl hadn't.

'If they're determined to do this, can we use it to draw the thing out, sir?' suggested Josh quietly to the inspector. 'At least, if he attacks in the morning, we'll be able to see what we're dealing with.'

'I refuse to be used as bait!' Melissa was indignant.

'Then let us take care of the crown,' repeated the inspector wearily. 'Better still, let us drive you all home. Get you away from the danger.'

'No!' snapped Melissa. She knew she was being unreasonable, but somehow, she couldn't stop herself.

'Very well,' said the inspector, standing up to leave. 'I can't force you to change your minds, but I think you're all mad.'

****

Chapter Sixteen

Melissa lay in bed staring at the ceiling. She'd been awake for most of the night, while Mike slept solidly beside her. She knew she was acting irrationally, hanging onto the crown and entering the Cosplay Competition, when the police didn't want her to, but she couldn't help it. She was always the dominant one in their group, the one who made the decisions, and she was well aware that the others thought she could be bossy. They didn't understand that she really *needed* to be in control.

When she was a child she'd been bullied, and sometimes beaten, by her father, and eventually taken away from him and placed in care. Bounced from pillar to post between care homes and foster placements all she wanted to do was grow up, get out and take control of her own life. She'd worked hard to do it and created a fresh start for herself. She told her friends and colleagues that her family lived abroad, and she didn't see them much, and they all assumed she'd had the same experiences that they'd had growing up.

Her bossiness, as they called it, was because as a child, her father had taken a cruel delight in disappointing her. He'd promise her a treat and then deliberately cancel their plans or buy her a present and then withhold it for months or give it away to somebody else. That was *before* he started beating her; things only got worse after that. It left Melissa with a dogged determination to always do what she intended. Not to let anyone or anything spoil her plans. The only time she'd ever cancelled a social arrangement was when Mike needed her support when his grandmother died, and she'd chosen to do that; nobody had made her.

So now she was choosing to carry on at Geek Camp, enter the Cosplay Competition and act as if nothing was happening. It was a kind of coping strategy. If she pretended that nothing was wrong, then perhaps the world would get back on track and nothing *would* be wrong.

She tried not to think about Alec and Jess at the hospital, even though she was genuinely fond of both of them. One thing she'd had to learn young was the art of detachment. As early as she reasonably could, she crept out of bed, showered, and began to get into her Galadriel cosplay.

****

Artie and Emily were staring at Jamie's second cosplay in admiration. He'd bought a gold body suit and then used EVA foam to create all the joints, face mask and helmet of C3PO from Star Wars. He'd even made a stomach plate with the robot's wiring running down it. He'd sprayed all the pieces gold except for his left arm, which was dark red.

'That is fantastic!' said Emily.

'I'm seriously impressed,' added Artie.

'Well,' said Jamie, delighted with their reaction, 'I knew you were going to cosplay as Rey, Emily, so I thought I'd create the version of C3PO that appears in The Force Awakens, where he's wearing the arm of a fellow droid who died to save him, as a sign of friendship.'

Emily smiled. She felt that she and Jamie were just beginning to move beyond friendship now, and it felt good. She had put together a light grey cosplay, with knee length trousers, a sleeveless vest-top, ridged arm wraps and brown ankle boots. With two very long grey cotton scarfs crossing over at the front and back, held in place by a double strap belt with a rough brown bag attached, and her long brown hair tied back, she looked very like the character played by Daisy Ridley in the Star Wars film.

Luke and Katy joined them, wearing the same cosplays as the day before, though Luke swore that as soon as they'd had some greenscreen photos taken, he was going to get out of his cosplay and back into normal clothes.

'I can't do another whole day as a Dalek! It's way too uncomfortable.'

'I love that look, Emily,' said Katy. 'And the bag.'

'Oh yes,' agreed Emily smiling. 'Time for a cosplay with pockets, or a bag, to put stuff in.'

'That's one of the advantages of a lab coat,' Katy laughed, 'Pockets.'

'Are you sure you're up for this, Jamie?' Artie asked his friend. 'We can all change our minds, if anyone wants to.'

'After the amount of work, I've put into this cosplay?' said Jamie. 'But we're all agreed? We stick together the whole time, no wandering off doing our own thing?' They all nodded and set off for the main venues.

As they got to the open area in front of the venues, they stopped to watch The Galactic Knights running their Orc Boot Camp. The Orcs looked amazing, and menacing, but the children they were working with were unfazed, as they were taught orc attack and defence strategies and how to protect themselves behind a shield formation. After taking a few photos, and enjoying watching the Orcs at work, the group moved on to the Moon Base to take part in the Cosplay Prelims. The space was packed with people, but although the group of friends were all on the alert, none of them could spot a dark elf. Nor could Scott and Josh, the two Men in Black assigned to keep them safe.

****

Melissa, Mike and Lee were just about to leave their caravan when her mobile rang.

'Hi Mel, it's Jess. I thought you'd want to know. Alec's surgery went ok, and he's not in critical condition anymore. He's going to be ok.' Jess was weeping with relief at the other end of the call.

'That's great news,' said Mel. 'So, are you both coming back? We're about to go over to the Cosplay Competition.'

'Mel! Alec's still very badly injured. He won't be out of hospital for a week. Maybe more. I really don't think cosplay is that important right now.'

'Well, it's important to me!' snapped Mel. 'And you can't stay at the hospital forever, can you?' Mel's voice softened. 'I'm sorry Jess. Look, if you do come back to the site, come and find us. The police have said we should all stick together, for safety. Besides, if it's been that stressful, it might be good for you to be with friends. Give Alec our love.'

****

Chapter Seventeen

Jess wasn't sure how she could get back to the site, even if she had been ready to leave Alec. She'd travelled to the hospital in the ambulance with him, and she didn't even have any money on her to get back there in a taxi. It was the usual frustration of cosplay – no pockets. She had had a tenner stuck into her modest cleavage the day before, but she'd spent that in the bar, and never got back to the caravan to collect more cash. The nurses were kindly letting her sit beside Alec's bed, at least until he was fully conscious. She didn't want him to wake up alone after what he'd been through. As she watched him sleep, she thought he looked younger than he did usually. Less anxious. Well, anaesthetics will do that to a person.

With the wig removed Alec seemed more like his everyday self. His mousey brown hair was looking untidy against the pillow. She reached forward to brush a strand of it off his high forehead. She knew he worried about having a receding hairline, but she'd known him for three years and he still looked the same as when she met him. What did it matter anyway? It wouldn't change who he was, not for her.

She wondered what he'd say if he ever found out that she liked him. Really liked him. She had sometimes speculated whether what she felt for him was just a crush, but after the attack the night before she knew it wasn't. She would have risked her own life, if she could, to save his, and she was pretty sure that wasn't how people felt about a crush.

One of the local policemen popped his head around the door.

'How's he doing?' he asked.

'Out of danger,' Jess replied. 'Though he hasn't come around yet. He'll be in hospital for a while though.'

'I've brought Simon in for treatment,' replied the policeman. 'We'll be some time, I think. He'll need his hand x-rayed and the bones set properly. I'll come back when we're done, and if you're ready to leave then I can give you a lift back to the site. One of our team will be staying here though, to keep an eye on your friend.'

Jess nodded her thanks and turned back to look at Alec as the policeman left. He was just beginning to stir, and before long he opened his eyes and smiled at her, then winced in pain as he discovered that any movement hurt.

'Hello Jess,' his said, his voice weak. 'What happened? I had the strangest dream.' He glanced down at his chest and saw the bandages, felt the pain. 'It was a dream, wasn't it?'

'I'm afraid not,' Jess replied. 'Not if was about some strange elf creature attacking us and taking your Elrond crown. He nearly killed all of us. It was terrifying.'

'Yep,' said Alec. 'That was the dream.' He tried to sit up but fell back against the pillows as waves of pain flooded over him. 'Did he hurt you? Is that why you're here?'

'Just a few bruises,' replied Jess, shaking her head. 'I'm fine. I just couldn't bear to leave you here on your own. You nearly died last night. The doctors said that thing ripped through your skin and into some of your organs. Not your heart, luckily, or you wouldn't be here. I thought I'd lost you.' Deciding that was a bit too much like a declaration she back tracked, 'I mean, we could have lost you.' He reached his hand towards her gently and placed it on top of her hand on the bed covers, too tired to respond in any other way. As he drifted off to sleep, he heard Jess mutter, 'And the next time someone tries to take a piece of your cosplay, just let them, alright?'

****

The Cosplay Preliminaries were underway when Mel, Mike and Lee arrived. Lee was still refusing to enter the competition, although he was wearing his Thorin Oakenshield cosplay.

A very tired, and possibly hung-over Host was jollying everyone along, and sorting them into categories. He'd chosen a different outfit for the day, a suit covered in pineapples, mainly because his Joker cosplay tended to frighten the children, and there were quite a few child entries. While waiting for his turn, Jamie had taken his helmet off to cool down, and the Host recognised him as the hobbit from the night before. He went over to Jamie and whispered to him.

'Did last night really happen? Or had I just had too much to drink?'

'It happened,' Jamie whispered back, 'Every terrifying moment of it.'

The Host groaned and moved over to the police escorts, trying to get them to enter the competition as a Men in Black group cosplay. Henry and Stan refused, politely, although Josh and Scott were just a little tempted. The two of them had already decided that they wanted to try and come to the event the following year, as regular attendees, provided they could book the time off work.

The Prelims were judged by a group of Guest Cosplayers, who always enjoyed working at this particular event. At some conventions the cosplayers could be wildly competitive, sometimes putting each other down just to win a competition, but at Geek Camp the cosplayers were generally good natured. Some people were competitive, others just cosplayed for fun, and there wasn't too much drama around the competition, however keen some people were to win it.

Each entrant had to walk on to the stage, strike a pose and walk off, and the judges had to whittle about forty cosplayers down to fifteen. Mel and Mike got through to the Final, as did Jamie in his C3PO cosplay. Luke had already decided not to enter the competition. He really didn't want to be stuck as a Dalek all day, and he was happy enough just to enjoy being in cosplay round the site without feeling he needed to compete. That way he could change into something more comfortable later. Katy didn't enter either so she, Artie and Lee stood together and cheered on their friends. Emily didn't get through, which they all thought was a shame, but she didn't mind too much. She was just really proud that Jamie had made it to the Final.

Artie decided that maybe he would have a go at cosplay next year, after chatting to another Finalist, a Lady Loki with long dark hair who was wearing a green tunic with a broad criss-crossed leather waistband-cum-belt. Her outer robe was green, with leather panels riveted onto it and her boots were laced and reached above her knees. She'd completed her cosplay with a wire horned crown and a staff with triple blades made from EVA foam and topped off with a blue stone. Artie thought her craftsmanship was amazing, and that it might be fun to create all his own props, even if he didn't enter the competition.

The Prelims finished with the children's Cosplay Competition. There was a family group cosplaying as the Hogwarts's Train, a baby Chewbacca, little witches and characters from Toy Story, all taking part. For them this was a single competition – there was no way anyone could expect the younger ones to still be awake and in cosplay by the evening, so they weren't expected to take part in the Final. The Host was a little quieter and gentler with the children. The last thing he wanted was to be too over the top, freak them out and put them off cosplay for life.

As soon as the Prelims were finished Artie hurried all of his friends off to the smallest venue, the Satellite Zone to see a one-woman sci-fi puppet show called "Behind the Sofa". It was a pastiche of a lot of popular tv shows and movies, and the performer involved different members of the audience at various points in the story. The woman was small and plump, with mid-length wavy brown hair, and wore a long coat created to look like an exploding Tardis. She leapt about the stage grabbing the puppets she needed at various moments in the story. Artie looked at the ones she had built and decided he wanted to add puppet building to his skills.

The audience was a real mix of people, from the podcaster Dr Squee, who was sitting beside a charming looking woman with long blond hair and an enormous smile, to families with young children, alongside adults in Star Trek Uniforms, some of whom eagerly volunteered to take part when a member of the Enterprise crew was called for. The girl who'd been wearing a cosplay from The Handmaid's Tale the night before was there too, this time wearing a brilliant red leather outfit and with blue hair, cosplaying as Illyria from Angel. Presumably it was easier to see what was going on without the deep bonnet, and beside her sat an older woman with short dark hair, both enjoying the performance. Children got involved in the action too, a rather cute brother and sister coming onstage to help the central character catch a monster.

The sound desk was being operated by a man was in his late fifties, big and bearded, with fair hair turning silver-blond and smiling blue-grey eyes. He wasn't in cosplay and Artie guessed he was the performer's husband, who had obviously come along to help with the show. Luke and Katy loved the performance, which had a strong Whovian theme.

As "Behind the Sofa" finished the group headed off, by agreement, to get greenscreen photos taken. They chose Dr Who or Star Wars images as backgrounds, and also had a big group shot of all of them, Artie included, taken on the deck of the Enterprise, from Star Trek. They even persuaded Scott and Josh to pose for a proper Men in Black background shot, and all of them started giggling, especially when the policemen both took up a fighting stance for one picture, with tasers in one hand and horseshoes in the other, but refused to explain why.

Katy insisted that they went to one of the stalls that sold jewellery so that she could buy a Whovian-Steampunk style necklace that she'd seen the day before. It was made up of cogs and wheels and little brass charms of a Tardis and its key, along with a miniature bowtie and a tiny metal stripy scarf like the one she was wearing.

Artie was looking a bit pale, even if he had been smiling for the photographs, and was prepared to wait patiently while his friends shopped. He was reluctant to admit it, but his chest, and what he suspected was his heart, were hurting. It was probably just bruising from the night before, but Jamie saw his friend's face, and suggested that they all went and sat down in the Star Base to watch the interview with Frazer Hines, who had played Jamie McCrimmon in the early days of Dr Who. The actor was a frequent visitor to Geek Camp, and was always popular, so the group were quite relieved to find seats where they, and their police buddies, could all sit together. Jamie's cosplay felt tight over the bandages on his chest, and he too was glad of the chance to have a rest. The interview was interesting, with Frazer talking about working with Patrick Troughton, the second Doctor. He could do a great impression of his old friend too, and it turned out that he was recording a lot of classic doctor who audios with Big Finish. The whole group, police team included, settled down to enjoy the interview.

****

The Prelims over Henry and Stan, the police team that were protecting Melissa and her friends, headed over to join them, intending to collect Mel's Galadriel crown and lock it safely in the room the inspector was using as an office, until the evening. All three of the Lord of the Rings cosplayers had been surrounded by photographers asking to take pictures, even though Lee hadn't entered the contest. Their cosplays really were impressive. One of the official photographers, the long-haired man, finished his photos and stepped back to allow other attendees to take their pictures.

Meanwhile the female photographer, who had already captured images of the Lord of The Rings group the night before, was trying to encourage Henry and Stan to pose for a Men in Black shot before moving away. She succeeded in convincing them to strike a couple of poses, and the two policemen grinned at each other. This really was the oddest surveillance job they'd ever been given.

When the crowd finally cleared around the group, the policemen realised they had a problem. Mike and Lee were still there, but there was no sign of Melissa.

'She's probably just slipped off to the ladies,' Mike said reassuringly. 'She'll be back in a minute.'

'When the inspector said none of you were to go anywhere alone,' snapped Stan, his good mood evaporating in an instant, 'He meant *anywhere*. We need to find her, straight away.' They all headed for the Ladies toilets in the corner of the venue, but they had been closed for cleaning. Which meant that Melissa must have left the building on her own to find alternative toilets. The policemen groaned, and Henry put in a call to the inspector.

****

Chapter Eighteen

Melissa hadn't meant to ignore the police escort. She didn't think she needed to let them know she was just going to the ladies. Not when it was only a few feet away. When she reached the toilets and discovered they were closed, she completely forgot that she'd cause a panic by simply disappearing. She was so thrilled to have got through to the Final of the Cosplay Competition. She'd worked really hard to create the dress, and she knew her whole cosplay looked stunning. She was busy deciding what she and Mike should do during the Final. They were meant to do more than just strike a pose for that. They could act out a little dialogue in character, or perhaps perform a dance to a snippet of the film score, something elegant and graceful which would be fitting for Galadriel and Legolas; so long as Mike wasn't feeling too self-conscious.

Knowing that there was often a queue for the toilets in the Star Base, she opted to use the ones in the games area. They were tucked down a side corridor and she was delighted to see that there wasn't a queue there, in fact there wasn't anyone around at all. As she entered the area where the wash basins were, she noticed a shadow suddenly appear up on the windowsill, on the other side of the glass. A strangely shaped shadow clutching a long staff. Realising how foolish she'd been, she turned and ran, out of the toilets and along the corridor. She heard the sound of smashing glass, as the dark elf broke the window with his staff and threw himself in through it, and she turned. Behind her was the creature the inspector had warned her about, and a couple of hundred yards ahead was the games area, and the safety in numbers that came from being amongst people.

Thankful she'd chosen flat shoes, Mel sprinted towards the room ahead of her. Suddenly she found she couldn't move. Something was transfixing her to the spot. She tried to open her mouth to scream, but no sound came out.

Ramilid stalked around her, savouring the moment. He could feel the power in her crown, even before he reached out to rip it from her head. He was taken aback when he found her long hair came off too, attached to the crown by hair clips. Removing the wig made her fake elf ears much more visible, and Ramilid felt a tide of anger rising inside him. This mortal had dared to wear the crown of one of the queens of the Fae. She was standing before him wearing false ears, pretending to be one of *his* people. She may not have stolen the crown in the first place, but to him her offence seemed almost as great.

Unable to move, Mel stared at Ramilid in horror. Even now, she couldn't really process what she was seeing. A tiny part of her brain wanted to demand that he gave her the crown and wig back – how could she enter the Final without them? Most of her brain was screaming at her that the Cosplay Competition really wasn't that important, and the main thing was just to stay alive. Looking into the dark elf's eyes, she realised that wasn't very likely to happen.

She recognised that look. She'd seen it in her father's eyes when she was a child. The look of somebody who wanted to punish for punishment's sake, of a man who enjoyed using his strength, his power, to subdue those who were weaker than he was. Unable to move, she knew that she couldn't escape, or protect herself. The only way she could fight back was to refuse to give him the satisfaction of seeing her fear. It was a technique she'd learned as a young girl, and sometimes, just sometimes, it had worked; deflected the anger, calmed the storm. She took a deep breath and steadied herself, trying to make her face neutral, peaceful even, hoping that it would de-escalate the situation and cause her attacker to withdraw. After all, he'd got what he came for, there was no need to continue the attack on her. Unfortunately, it didn't work.

Ramilid raised his staff and brought it crashing down on her head, splitting her skull open. In his rage he would have chosen to give her a more painful death, but there was no time for his style of poetic justice. He could be discovered at any moment, and although he now had both the stone and the wreath, there was still another task he had to undertake.

****

By the time the police found Melissa's body, Ramilid was gone, taking the crown and the wig with him. He'd ripped off her false ears before he left too, leaving one of her earlobes hanging off. It seemed unnecessarily cruel to the inspector, who stared down at her mutilated corpse in horror. Her blood was soaking into the beautiful elven gown that she spent so many hours creating, desecrating it. He found himself oddly sad that she'd never have her chance to take part in the competition she'd been so looking forward to. It wasn't the kind of thing that would matter to him, but he knew it had been important to her, and it seemed tragic that her hopes, as well as her life, had been snatched away from her.

He blamed himself, inevitably. He should have just confiscated the crown when he had the chance. Realistically he was aware that the elf would then just have attacked whoever had the crown, and that either himself or one of his team would have died instead. But then, that was what the police were there for, wasn't it? To take the risks in order to protect other people ... and they'd failed. He'd failed. In truth he had no idea how to stop the creature. It wasn't the kind of situation he'd ever expected to come across. He asked Henry, his constable, to go and find some fabric to cover her with. That shouldn't be difficult at an event filled with cosplayers. He felt that the least he owed her was respect, and he didn't want to leave her corpse exposed on the floor for everyone to stare at.

****

When the interview was over, many of the audience hurried away to get photographs and autographs with Frazer Hines. Artie, however dragged all of his friends over to the Book Base. The couple who ran the base were there, along with the stalwart family that helped them with the bookselling, but there were other authors too. Artie saw the woman who'd been performing "Behind the Sofa" was doing a book signing. Apparently, she was a writer too. He wandered over to chat to her about puppet building, and the others browsed the book stall. There several authors there, signing and selling their books, and Artie couldn't resist spending far more money than he'd planned, but then he always did at Geek Camp. He ended up back talking to Sam, the woman who ran the Book Base. He'd already got all of her steampunk novels, but she wrote in so many different genres that he thought he'd try some of her other books. He picked up her new thriller, and one of her collections of horror stories, and dug out his card to pay, before packing about a dozen newly signed books into the rucksack he'd brought with him to carry them.

When he turned around, he saw that something was wrong. His friends had finished their book shopping before he had, and were grouped around their policemen, looking shocked. He hurried over to join them, to discover that Josh and Scott, their police escorts, had had a message to escort them all to the inspector's temporary office at once. Seeing how serious the officers looked, nobody argued.

****

Chapter Nineteen

They reached the office to find the inspector waiting for them. Mike and Lee, who they'd been chatting to that morning, were there too. Mike was trying hard not to cry, and his friend was attempting to comfort him. Simon's friend Bella was sitting out of the way, in a corner, waiting for him to return from the hospital.

'I'm sorry to give you all bad news,' explained the inspector, 'But as these three already know, the creature has struck again. I'm afraid it killed Melissa. We assume it was because she had the crown he was after. I want to apologise, to all of you. I'd said we'd try to keep you safe, and we failed.'

There was silence as everyone absorbed the news, then Bella leaned forward and spoke to the inspector.

'You didn't fail,' she said. 'None of this should have happened, but it wasn't your fault. You've tried to protect all of us. You wanted everyone to leave, but we wouldn't, and even if we had, that creature would just have followed people home and attacked them anyway. And it's not as if the police are trained to deal with something like this. He's not a normal criminal.'

The inspector smiled at her, grateful to have someone on his side, trying to lift the guilt he was feeling, but it was still his responsibility.

'I have no idea how to catch the killer,' he admitted. 'Maybe now he's got the objects he came for; he'll just go back to where he came from.' He gave Mike and Lee an apologetic glance. 'I know that's not the same as bringing someone to justice, making him pay for what he did to Melissa, and everyone else he's attacked, but at least it would mean you were all safe.'

'I don't think he'll just go,' said Bella. 'For a start, there's another object. A chalice or something. Simon told him it was in the post, but it should have been delivered by now. Won't the creature go after that? Attack whoever bought it?'

The inspector reached into a drawer in the desk and pulled out a silver chalice embossed with gold filigree decoration, sitting on top of its wrappings.

'That's why I sent one of my officers to collect it first thing this morning. Simon gave me the address. So hopefully that's one person who won't be attacked, as the creature doesn't know where she lives.'

'Doesn't that mean that he'll come after Simon again? To get the address?' Bella queried.

The inspector nodded, unable to fault her reasoning. How the hell was he supposed to end this? He couldn't catch the creature, and even if he did he wouldn't be able to arrest him, and bring him to trial for three murders and multiple assaults, and he was pretty sure no prison would be able to hold him if he did.

'I've got an idea,' said Bella.

****

Jess and Simon were being driven back from the hospital. Alec was resting and Jess felt that he was stable enough for her to leave him, for a few hours anyway. She couldn't understand why their friends hadn't come to the hospital to visit him, even if Mel was focused on the Cosplay Competition. Still, she had enjoyed having a little time alone with Alec. When he wasn't too drowsy, they'd chatted about all sorts of things, even his frustration at missing the rest of Geek Camp.

'I wish I'd bought the books I planned to get yesterday,' he said with a weak smile. 'I think I'll have plenty of time to read over the next few weeks.'

'Never mind,' said Jess. 'I'm just glad you're alive, and there's always next year – assuming this hasn't put you off forever.'

'Weirdly, it hasn't. What about you?'

'I'll come if you will,' she agreed with a smile. 'So long as we're sure that this is over.'

When the policeman pulled into the car park, Simon and Jess were led to the inspector's office and told the bad news. They both took it hard, Jess because Melissa was her best friend, and also because she'd felt really angry at Mel that morning for not being bothered about Alec, which made her feel guilty as well as grief-stricken.

Simon was distraught, blaming himself for everything.

'I'm sorry, I'm so sorry,' he was saying to Melissa's friends, over and over again. 'It's all my fault. I never meant for this to happen…….'

It was Bella who eventually managed to get him to calm down and listen to her idea.

'So, you want to use me as bait?' Simon responded when he finally understood what she was getting at. Bella just nodded. There was nothing she could say to reassure him.

'Fair enough,' said Simon numbly, after a long silence. 'I started this. It should be me who tries to finish it. Besides, I'm pretty sure he'll come after me anyway, wherever I am. It might as well be out in the open.'

'I can't guarantee your safety,' said the inspector, 'But I will try my best to protect you.'

Simon just nodded. Three people were dead, and others were injured. Even if he didn't survive another encounter with Ramilid, it was down to him to try and stop what he'd started. He wasn't sure he could live with the guilt anyway, so if there was anything, he could do that might help, he was up for it.

The inspector left the room to talk to the event organisers about what the police needed. When Melissa had been killed, he'd discussed with them whether the rest of the event should be cancelled immediately. The organisers thought everyone should be sent home, but the inspector felt that the subsequent panic might not be helpful and could even trigger the creature into attacking people who weren't connected to the objects he was seeking. He had advised them that it was safer to carry on as though nothing had happened and protect the remaining targets. He just hoped he was right.

****

Chapter Twenty

At the inspector's request, the organisers had shut the Treehouse Adventure Playground, and closed the curtains in the Satellite Zone so that visitors to the event couldn't look out into the playground and see what was happening. The treehouses were made up of a series of wooden towers, a little like the towers of a castle, linked by raised walkways of wood or rope. There was a flight of wooden steps going up and two big plastic slides angled down from a couple of the towers, one straight and one which was enclosed and formed a loop. Simon was sitting in the middle of a patch of open ground at the far end, clutching the chalice nervously. Forming a perfect circle round him was a ring of horseshoes, each touching the next, in the hope that the dark elf couldn't get into the centre of the circle. Bella had even insisted on adding a circle of salt around the outside, and then covered the circle in some bark chippings so that it blended in with the soft surface of the play area. She and Simon were the only non-police there.

The rest of the group had been left in the office under the protection of the two local police officers – just in case. The inspector tried to make Bella stay there too, but that was never going to happen. This was her plan, Simon was her friend, and she wasn't about to let Blake treat her like a delicate female who needed protecting. For some reason she was determined to impress him.

The inspector actually was quite impressed with Bella, not that he was going to give her the satisfaction of showing it. He thought she was brilliant and determined and a good person to have at your side in a crisis, but he wasn't at all sure her plan would work and he'd rather she hadn't insisted on putting herself in the danger zone. As it was, he insisted that she watch from the top of one of the towers, rather than wait at ground level.

It was mid-afternoon when Simon got into position and half an hour went past with no sign of the dark elf. The armed response team were tucked out of sight at the top of the towers, while the other officers were hidden in the shadows between the supports at the bottom of the treehouses. They were all beginning to think that nothing was going to happen. Even Simon began to relax, very slightly.

While everyone was looking around to see if the dark elf would appear at the edge of the playground, the creature suddenly dropped down from above, landing squarely beside Simon. Ramilid had used a glamour to prevent himself from being seen on the roof of the Satellite Zone, until he jumped down next to his target. The inspector swore under his breath. The plan had been that the creature couldn't get too close to Simon because the elf couldn't cross the circle of iron around him. That would have given Simon a chance to negotiate his freedom in return for the chalice. Now, if Bella's theory was correct, the dark elf was trapped inside the circle with the two things it wanted. Simon *and* the chalice.

'Run Simon,' yelled Bella, jumping into the spiral slide that led from the top of the tower where she'd been placed, and spinning down to land in an untidy heap on the ground. 'Leave the chalice and run!'

It took Simon a moment to grasp what she was getting at, but a moment was all that Ramilid needed. The dark elf grabbed hold of Simon by his arm and snatched the silver cup from him.

'One task completed', the dark elf hissed. 'All that's left is to punish you, thief! A slow death for you, I think, and a painful one, in return for all the trouble you've caused me.'

With one hand he tucked the chalice into his bag, while retaining his grip on Simon, who was struggling to get away. This put just enough distance between him and Ramilid for the inspector to give the order to his men.

'Now!' he called, and two of the armed response team fired at the dark elf. The creature just laughed.

'Your bullets can't hurt me!' he said, an unpleasant smile on his face. 'Nor can those little electric guns of yours,' he added as several tasers were fired in his direction.

With the hand that had been holding the chalice now free, Ramilid clicked his fingers. Simon whimpered in panic and crows appeared in the air above the circle.

'Now,' called Bella.

Feeling incredibly foolish, the police team pulled horseshoes out of their pockets and flung them at the dark elf. These actually did seem to hurt him, and he twisted this way and that trying to avoid contact with weapons that were obviously painful to creatures of his kind. One of the horseshoes hit the hand the elf was using to hang on to Simon and he lost his grip. Simon took the opportunity to leap out of the circle, and Ramilid attempted to follow him, only to discover he was trapped within it, held there by the power of iron and of salt.

'You might have trapped me, but you can't keep me here forever,' he growled, 'And you can't stop me getting my revenge.' He gave a strange, guttural cry, and the crows that had been circling above began to descend, preparing to attack Simon.

Bella, who had spent most of the night researching folklore on her phone, remembered something she'd read about knowing a fairy's true name giving you power over them. She started chanting it just as the first few birds began to claw at her friend.

'Ramilid! Ramilid! Ramilid!' she shouted.

Soon the police officers joined in.

'Ramilid! Ramilid! Ramilid!' they yelled.

The inspector ran forward and threw his coat over Simon to give him some protection from the birds, but already they were pulling back from the attack. Chanting the dark elf's name seemed to be diminishing the magic he was using to control the crows. The inspector helped Simon to his feet, picked up his coat and led the young man away from the circle, over to where Bella was standing.

'What now?' the inspector asked her.

'No idea,' replied Bella. 'Just keep chanting until we think of something?'

'Ramilid! Ramilid! Ramilid!' The inspector and Simon joined in with the chanting.

After ten minutes they were getting hoarse, and Bella hadn't come up with any way out of the impasse. She was worried that if they all kept chanting for hours, they'd lose their voices and Ramilid would be free to attack them again somehow, even if he was still trapped in the circle.

'Thank you, mortals,' said a gentle voice from behind them. 'You may stop chanting now. You're giving us a headache.'

They turned around to find that while they had been focused on the middle of the playground, some more elves had appeared behind them. For a moment they were afraid that Ramilid had summoned assistance, and that they were about to be under attack, but one glance told them these creatures were completely different to the dark elf who'd been causing them so much trouble.

'Greetings from the Seelie Court,' announced the ethereal creature in front of them. 'I believe you have something that belongs to us.' Simon hoped that they didn't mean him.

****

Chapter Twenty-One

Ramilid's face fell. This was the last thing he'd expected or wanted. The Seelie and Unseelie Courts were not exactly enemies, more like two sides of the same coin; but in this case opposites did not attract, and they generally avoided contact with each other.

The humans stared at the new arrivals in amazement. More elves. Pale elves? Light elves? They weren't sure quite how to describe them but were relieved that they looked much less threatening than the creature they had been battling. While Ramilid was dark and menacing, these elves were pale in their dress and colouring. Blake thought sadly that Melissa would have loved to achieve that delicate look in her Galadriel cosplay. Some of them appeared to be female and some were male. All of their robes were long and seemed almost to float around them, giving them the appearance of shimmering. Even their skin had a glistening silver sheen and each of their wooden staffs, which were all different in appearance, emitted a soft glow. Their wings hung down their backs, silver at the shoulders with the colour fading downwards until it only showed in the veins which could be seen through the transparent membranes.

Stan, who was a keen wildlife watcher when he was off duty, thought that they looked like the wings of cicadas. He tried to whisper this information to Henry, but the younger officer just stared at the light elves, transfixed.

'You may go,' said the pale female who appeared to be the leader of the group, inclining her head towards the humans.

'I'm afraid it's not as simple as that,' the inspector replied. 'This creature has killed three people and injured several others. Under our laws, I need to arrest him.'

'You would never be able to hold on to him,' she said smoothly. 'I am Sylvatica - Enforcer of the Seelie Court. You may leave him in my charge.'

The inspector was trying hard not to feel intimidated, which was remarkably difficult, when faced with half a dozen light elves. However, he was responsible for dealing with the situation. He couldn't just walk away.

'There is such a thing as the chain of command; the rules of custody.' He was struggling to put his thoughts into words. 'I would need to know more, about you *and* your courts. Will he be released to cause further harm, or will be punished, and if so, how? I can no more send him to his death than allow him to simply go free.'

'Such scruples,' said Sylvatica with a slight smile. 'Very well, I shall explain. We are a different part of creation to you mortals, or to the heavenly beings – we live by different rules and possess different powers – old powers. At the beginning of time, some of the angels chose to rebel, to fall, to take demon form and begin an endless battle with the Creator. We of the Fae did not. Those of *our* kind simply - drifted away.'

Blake tried to grapple with the idea of heavenly beings, of angels and demons, actually existing - and decided to worry about that later. His brain couldn't handle any more shocks at the moment.

'We found we were far more attracted to the world that was created, than to the One who created it.' Sylvatica continued, 'We were allowed to choose, and we chose we did. But there were conditions. We were to do no harm in the human world, nor interfere with it, so long as no-one interfered with us. This allowed us to live in our own way, flying under the radar of humans and of the rest of creation.'

'That sounds idyllic,' said Belle wistfully.

'It was, for a time' Sylvatica agreed. 'But we, too, fell into disputes. Eventually we diverged and split into two courts - the Seelie Court, governed by the light elves, and the Unseelie, belonging to the dark. Our courts have different rules and attitudes.'

'I still don't know why I'm supposed to just hand my prisoner over to you,' said the inspector.

'Because he has broken our laws, as well as yours, by bringing our world to your attention,' she replied. 'As Enforcer, he was tasked to retrieve the stolen Hoard – but it belonged to *our* court, not his. While he *might* have been able to justify punishing the thieves, especially as they had also broken your human laws by failing to report their find ...' Her eyes rested on Simon and he began to squirm, 'He had no right to attack or kill other humans. Once he had murdered that girl today, who had *no* connection to the theft, we were empowered to act, but we were not sure where he was hiding until you drew him out into the open and summoned us by chanting his name, for which assistance, much thanks.'

'I still need to know what you're planning to do with him!' The inspector was adamant.

'He shall be tried before both our courts, and I expect, imprisoned - eternally. No pain, no torture, no death - just endless boredom and frustration. For a creature with eternity ahead of him, it's a surprisingly unpleasant existence. One where he can do no further harm to your people or to mine. We shall take Ramilid, and the Hoard, into our custody and turn both over to the two courts in our realm, to determine his punishment, and the true ownership of the Hoard.'

The inspector shrugged, feeling defeated. He couldn't see any option other than to hand the prisoner over.

'Wait,' he said. 'I want your word that none of you will come after this young man.' He pointed to Simon. 'He's been punished enough; he will not make the same mistake twice.'

Sylvatica looked Simon up and down contemptuously, then nodded.

'Very well,' she agreed coldly, although Simon didn't think she sounded even remotely sincere. 'Now give us our prisoner.' Seeing their puzzled expressions, she explained, 'Release him from the iron circle. We can no more cross it or handle it than he can.'

At a nod from the inspector, Josh and Scott moved towards the circle and created a gap in the horseshoes. All this time Ramilid had been standing inside it, with his head bowed, and a defeated look on his face. But he wasn't feeling defeated. Not at all. From the moment he had added the chalice to his shoulder bag to join the rest of the artefacts from the Hoard, he had sensed a gentle surge in power coming from within the satchel. As if putting all the objects back together increased the power of each. As the elf nearest to the Hoard, he realised that it was in turn gradually enhancing his powers, boosting his magic, extending his reach.

****

Now Ramilid leapt out of the circle, bowling the nearest policemen over, and raised his arm, clicking his fingers and calling the still circling crows down on everybody, but especially on the light elves.

He could feel his powers extending further, allowing him to call more and more crows, and ordering all of them to attack. Finding that he still had plenty of power available the dark elf called up tendrils from the earth, wrapping them round the police officers. Some of the shoots even twisted and climbed up the treehouses to ensnare the members of the armed response unit. These plants were bigger and stronger than the ones which had held Artie the night before, but even controlling both the vegetation and the crows, he found that he still had more resources.

Enraged by the interference of the light elves, he decided to extend his revenge. He reached out to *all* those he'd had direct contact with that were still within range, sensing most of them in the office nearby. Suddenly the outside wall of the office was licked by flames, the room began to fill with smoke and everyone in it had to escape by running outside. Once they were in the open air Ramilid compelled those of them he could identify to come towards him. The police officers were busy helping to deal with the fire and Katy, Luke, Mike and Lee had had no direct contact with the dark elf, but Artie, Jamie, Jess and Emily were irresistibly drawn towards where the struggle was taking place.

COLD DEAD COSPLAY

Even the Host felt a strange sensation, as though he was supposed to go 'somewhere' but at that moment he had to leap onstage to introduce the next guest at the event, and stage discipline, with its associated adrenaline rush, was stronger than the sensation compelling him. Like all good performers, he carried on with the show.

****

Chapter Twenty-Two

At first Sylvatica and the other light elves were as taken aback as the humans on the scene. Nobody had realised the implications of having all the pieces of the Hoard back in one place - and of that place being in the control of the dark elf. Distracted by the battering of the crows, who were pecking and clawing at them, it took the light elves a few minutes to begin to exert their own powers. Unable to counteract Ramilid's control over the birds completely and simply send them away, the light elves called down hailstones, to batter the crows into retreating. To the humans caught up in this battle, this felt almost as painful, but it was admittedly less frightening.

The inspector was trying to shelter Bella and Simon from the attack by dragging them towards him and pulling his coat over all of their heads, but they were held in place by the shoots that had grown up from the earth and twisted around them, pulling them embarrassingly close. The other police officers were just as trapped, and as confused. Scott felt blood trickling down his face from a gash inflicted by a particularly aggressive crow, and Josh, Stan and Henry were trying to free their arms to flap them at the birds who seemed determined to peck at their eyeballs. Nobody had expected to be caught up in this level of supernatural battle.

Jamie, Artie, Emily and Jess arrived just as the crows were starting to feel the effects of the hailstones and retreat, and the light elves stopped the hailstorm moments later.

Ramilid looked around at them all in satisfaction. The police were held in place by roots and shoots, and they and the light elves were cut and shaken by the birds that had attacked them. The dark elf decided to leave his revenge on Simon until last, instead he reached out a finger to beckon Jamie towards him. Even though the young man didn't want to get any closer, he found that he couldn't resist and began to step forward. Artie leapt in front of Jamie, trying to protect his friend, just as Jess and Emily grabbed Jamie by the arms to stop him moving.

'Leaping in to defend your friends again, young man?' Ramilid laughed. 'Remember what happened last time?' The dark elf reached out his hand towards Artie and clenched his fist.

'I shall destroy each of you in turn,' said Ramilid, with relish. 'You have all created obstacles for me, and now I have the power to make you regret it.'

Again, Artie felt a terrible pressure round his heart, which was contracting even more tightly this time. He stumbled forward and fell to the ground, just as Simon gave a howl of rage and despair and succeeded in breaking free of the tendrils holding him in place. He charged towards Ramilid at such speed that he managed to knock the dark elf over.

'No more killings!' yelled Simon. 'My mistake, my fault. No one else is going to die. Kill me!'

'With pleasure!' snarled Ramilid as he scrambled back onto his feet. He reached out his hand, snapped his fingers and his staff appeared in it. The ovoid shape at the top of the staff now seemed to pulse with power, strengthened by the magic of the Hoard. Even the dead beetle clinging to Ramilid's ear seemed to twitch as Simon stared at it in dismay. Before the dark elf could bring the staff down on Simon's head, the light elves, taking advantage of the distraction Simon had caused, attacked Ramilid.

Sylvatica made a wide gesture with her staff which cut through the straps of the bag containing the Hoard like a laser beam. It fell to the ground between Simon and Ramilid, and it was Simon who reached it first, and hurled it towards the light elves. Too stressed to aim well, it fell to the ground near the inspector, who succeeded in getting one arm and part of his upper body free from the tendrils to reach down and fling the bag to Sylvatica.

Suddenly Ramilid found himself enclosed in a ball of light, projected by the elves of the Seelie Court, each of whom was aiming a staff at him. Luminescence appeared to crackle from their staff tips to the globe of light encasing him. He tried to pierce the ball with his staff, and battered at it with his fists, but he couldn't burst it or fight his way out. Of course, it was now the light elves that were having their powers enhanced by possession of the Hoard, and there was no way he could win against them.

With Ramilid trapped, he could no longer sustain his control over the tendrils, which withered and sank back into the soil, releasing the police officers, as well as Bella and the inspector. Artie lay on the ground groaning, thankful to be free of the pain the dark elf had been inflicting. He was trying shake his head to flick his long fringe out of his eyes, but he didn't have the strength.

'You idiot!' whispered Jamie, kneeling beside his friend, and gently brushing Artie's fringe to one side. 'What did you go and do that for? You could have been killed!'

'I was just trying to protect you,' wheezed Artie. 'It's what friends do, isn't it? Besides, I didn't want him cutting you open again. It would have ruined your cosplay.'

'Are you prepared for us to take the prisoner now?' Sylvatic asked the inspector. He nodded. He'd seen that they could never contain the dark elf for any length of time. Frankly, the world was likely to be a safer place with the light elves in charge of Ramilid, rather than the police.

'Come prisoner!' Sylvatica commanded. 'Prepare to be judged by both your court and mine. I doubt you'll ever taste freedom again.'

'I'd rather die!' raged the dark elf. He reached down and snatched up three of the iron horseshoes that were still lying on the grass at his feet, although touching them obviously caused him pain. Holding them in one shaking hand and pointing his staff at them with the other, he shot flames at the metal until it began to soften and distort.

Then, as the light elves gasped in shock, he poured the molten iron down his throat.

Everyone watched in horror as he contorted in pain, before collapsing to the ground. The light elves dissolved the ball of light and rushed towards him, but there was nothing they could do. Ramilid had chosen to ingest liquid iron, and iron and Fae don't mix. As soon as the dark elf died his body began to shrink and whither to glistening dust. The dust blew away in the breeze and Ramilid was gone. All that remained was his staff.

Sylvatica picked it up and passed it to one of her fellows, then she turned to address the inspector.

'You are witness that he chose his own fate? It was not the punishment we would have delivered, but we had no part in his death?'

'I am witness,' agreed the inspector, formally.

'And you, young man,' she added, addressing Simon. 'You returned the Hoard to us willingly and would have sacrificed yourself for others. You will not be punished or pursued by any from our realms.' This time Sylvatica did sound sincere. 'But I do not expect you to search for treasure in future.' Simon nodded gratefully, unable to speak.

'What will happen to the Hoard?' asked Bella.

'That will be decided by our courts, I expect,' replied Sylvatica. 'Now we have seen its power when all the pieces are together, I can understand why it was hidden away in the earth. It would have been better for everyone, mortal and Fae, if it had remained there.'

With a final stern glance at Simon, she began to lead the party of light elves away. Before they had reached the treehouses, they vanished, leaving everyone uncertain about whether what they had just seen was real or - not.

The policemen breathed sighs of relief, despite ruefully examining their suits. The birds had ripped and clawed at the fabric, shredding it in places. Their faces too were battered and scratched; compared to what could have happened to them they all felt things could have been much, much worse. Scott even managed a grin.

'I don't think we could pass as the Men in Black anymore,' he said.

'More like Men in Rags,' agreed Josh.

'The paperwork on this case is going to be a nightmare,' muttered the inspector.

****

Chapter Twenty-Three

Everyone who had witnessed the events of the afternoon felt shaken, but they were terribly relieved that it was over. They all wandered back to the office to de-brief. Thankfully the fire had been extinguished quickly and had only damaged a small patch of one wall. Artie was relieved to see that his bag of books was still in one corner, unsinged.

The inspector filled in the other officers, along with Mike, Lee, Katy and Luke, on exactly what had happened that afternoon. He also suggested that people only talked about what they'd seen that day amongst themselves. No-one who hadn't seen it for themselves would believe them in any case; besides being laughed at wasn't going to help anyone.

'But Melissa's been murdered!' Mike protested.

'We can't just pretend that didn't happen,' Lee added.

'That goes for Maureen and Eddy too,' said Simon.

'Of course not.' The inspector looked at them all, wondering what to say. 'I suggest that you tell people that Melissa bought something that turned out to be stolen, then got murdered by the original owner trying to retrieve it. That person is now dead and nobody else is at risk. Simon, you could say the same about your friends, except you could say that you, Maureen and Eddy found the objects, if you wanted to.'

Everyone accepted the suggestion, reluctantly. Nobody wanted to gloss over what had happened, but they could see that the inspector had a point. He also insisted that Artie, and everyone who had been attacked by the crows, went to the hospital at once to get checked out and have their wounds properly treated.

'We just want to pack up our things and go home,' said Lee.

'It feels wrong staying on with Melissa being dead,' agreed Mike. 'How long will it take you to pack, Jess?'

'I don't know,' she replied. 'I mean I don't know about leaving. Alec's still in hospital. I want to go and see him again. I can't just leave him on his own. Maybe I'll stay on until tomorrow - although I don't fancy sleeping in our caravan on my own tonight.'

'Why don't you move into our van?' Emily offered. 'There's a spare bed in my room. Then you can visit your friend this evening and tomorrow morning, without being alone overnight.'

Jess accepted gratefully, but before helping to pack up their caravan, she had something else she needed to do. Collecting some money on the way she ran to the Book Base, where the steampunk author they'd seen interviewed the day before was just packing up his stall, which was on the next table along. She hurriedly bought some of his books, and a few others from the Book Base. The team there looked exhausted, but she supposed that as part of the group who organised the event, they must have known at least some of what had been going on, but had had to carry on as if nothing was wrong, which had to have been incredibly stressful.

It felt weird going shopping when her best friend had just been murdered, but the books weren't for her, and it felt important. A tiny positive thing to do in the middle of all the horror. Then she went to help Mike and Lee pack up the van. They agreed to take everyone's luggage back, including Mel's, and Jess changed out of her Arwen cosplay. It was a relief to shower and slip back into jeans after a day and a half in a medieval dress. She packed a change of clothes for Alec and a few bits and pieces for herself, piling the rest into Lee's car.

****

Jamie and Emily had insisted on accompanying Artie to the hospital. They were all a little scared that Ramilid might have done some permanent damage to his heart. While the inspector, Simon, Bella and the police officers were having their scratches and gashes properly cleaned, dressed and in Scott's case stitched, Artie was wired up to machines and tested. Not that they could tell the hospital staff exactly why they were so worried. The doctors found severe bruising, but no lasting damage, and insisted that Artie should rest for several days, and seek medical help if he began to feel worse.

Thankfully it was late afternoon on a quiet day in Spring, so they were all treated and released pretty quickly. The inspector took a few minutes to look in on Alec, explain what had happened to Melissa and reassure him that he was no longer in danger, though Alec seemed more concerned about Jess's safety.

****

It was almost seven o'clock when everyone got back to Geek Camp from the hospital. Katy and Luke had changed out of their cosplays and rustled up a meal for their friends, back at the van. They all had just enough time to shovel some food down before the evening events kicked off, but Jamie was more worried about his C3PO cosplay than about food. The events of the afternoon had loosened a couple of his EVA foam joints, and he'd forgotten to bring his hot glue gun with him.

'No worries,' said Artie with a grin. He opened the door of their caravan and shouted outside. 'Anyone got a hot glue gun we can borrow?' Within a minute two of the nearest vans had opened their doors and were offering glue guns, glue sticks, rivets, hammers and just about anything else a cosplayer could need. Jamie tried to repair his cosplay while wearing it, remembering a little late that that was a sure way to burn himself. Food eaten, cosplay mended, elbows and fingers burnt and repair kit returned; the group made their way over to the main venue to join the queue for the evening's events.

****

Mike and Lee were happy to take Jess to the hospital and see Alec themselves before they set off for home. It was a sombre visit. Alec was far more badly injured than Mike and Lee had realised, and now they were together again, they all felt Mel's absence more sharply. For the first time her death felt real, and final. The conversation ground to a halt.

'Let me know if you need anything when you get out of here,' said Mike, moving towards the door.

'Or if they move you closer to home,' added Lee.

'How will you get home, Jess?' asked Mike.

'I'll buy a train ticket when I'm ready to head back,' said Jess. 'The station isn't too far from the holiday park, I think'.

'Ok, well text one of us if you need picking up from the station tomorrow,' said Mike, and they were gone.

There was an awkward silence in the room, and Jess dug around in her bag and pulled out the books she'd bought.

'Here,' she said, piling them on the bedside cabinet. 'These are for you.'

'Thank you,' said Alec, giving her a grateful smile. 'I'm not sure if I can hold a book yet though. It hurts to move my arms.'

'Then I'll read to you until you fall asleep,' said Jess.

'That would be lovely,' said Alec smiling. 'But you can't stay here all night. Not two nights running.'

'I'll go back to Geek Camp later. I'll come and see you in the morning.' Seeing his troubled look, she added, 'It's alright. I'm staying with the other group, Jamie and Artie and their friends. I won't be alone.'

Alec nodded. He was too tired to speak, but despite everything that had happened, he felt a measure of contentment. Jess really must like him, at least a little, despite the age difference. He was horrified by Mel's death and had wept for her after the inspector left, but he couldn't help enjoying listening to Jess's voice, as she curled up in the uncomfortable hospital chair, opened the book she'd selected at the first page, and began to read.

****

Chapter Twenty-Four

Jamie and his friends had managed to get seats in the Star Base for the final evening of entertainment. Which was just as well, as his chest was beginning to throb again beneath the bandages, and Artie was looking very pale. They watched in delight as the Host, back in his Joker outfit, and beginning to look a little bit frazzled, introduced the rest of the entertainment team who performed a spectacular acrobatic dance routine to open to the evening. After that the Cosplay Competition Finalists were instructed to prepare to take their places. Jamie slid out of his seat and headed backstage, and each of the cosplayers in turn took to the stage and gave their performances.

Even though they were all rooting for Jamie, his friends had to admit that he was up against some incredible cosplays. There was a massive robot who needed the help of six people to get kitted up. His cosplay must have taken months to build, but it was well worth the effort for the effect it created. There were characters from fairy tales, fantasy and Sci-fi, and Artie recognised the Lady Loki he's spoken to earlier, as well as the others from the Preliminaries that morning.

Galadriel and Legolas were missing of course, although the Host glossed over why they weren't on stage. The thought of the lovely Galadriel he'd been chatting to that morning being murdered horrified him, as well as making him realise what a lucky escape he'd had the night before.

Jess squeezed her way into the venue just as the judges were getting into a huddle to choose the winner. She managed to weave her way over to where her new friends were sitting, wriggled past a bearded red-haired man on the end of the row, who was wearing a shirt covered in pineapples and holding a handmade puppet of the creator of The Dark Room, and slipped into Jamie's empty seat. By the time she'd filled them in on Alec the judges had called all the competing cosplayers back on stage to make their announcement. They were delighted when Jamie came third, and they stamped and cheered for him. Artie applauded when Lady Loki came a close second and everybody in the venue clapped for the winner, the enormous robot.

In the gap before the next event of the evening Luke and Katy nipped to the bar to buy a round of drinks and Jamie came back to re-join his friends. They had to shuffle up to fit six of them on five chairs, but it was manageable. Jamie found himself beside Emily, who kissed him on his foam cheek to congratulate him. He removed his helmet and gloves before he melted in the heat, took the drink Luke had brought him, and smiled. He felt Emily tuck her hand into his as they all settled down to enjoy The Dark Room.

****

The inspector had made sure that everything to do with the police investigation on the site was wrapped up. Melissa's body had been removed some hours before, but he had had a final conversation with the organisers and apologised for the burnt wall on the outside of the office, and the damage to the surface of the adventure playground. While he couldn't be completely honest with them about what had been going on, they realised that something very strange had happened, and were just thankful that it was over and done with.

He'd called his police officers together for a final briefing before sending them home. He made sure that none of them were too shaken up or badly injured to drive and promised to put the wheels in motion to put in a claim for their damaged suits.

That done, he went to find Simon and Bella, who'd been getting something to eat in the pub restaurant on the site and offered to drive them home.

'Not until you've had something to eat yourself,' said Bella firmly, thrusting the menu in front of him. 'You haven't stopped all day, and I can't remember when I last saw you eat anything.'

Blake felt that he should point out that he was in charge, and wasn't about to be bossed around by her; somehow, he didn't have the energy. He ordered food and a coffee, and they all sat and ate quietly.

Eventually Simon nerved himself to ask the inspector a question.

'When I get home, will ... Maureen and Eddy ... they won't still be there, will they?'

'No,' said the inspector, trying to sound reassuring. 'Their bodies have been removed and I had our clean up team go in. Your front door's been temporarily secured too. I can't guarantee that there won't be any signs of what happened, but you won't be walking back into what you left a couple of days ago.'

'Thank you,' Simon smiled, nervously. 'I was dreading going back.'

'I can't take away the memories, I'm afraid,' said the inspector. 'And I'll need to you come into the station to give a full statement on Monday, but other than that, the worst is over.'

'You can sleep at mine tonight Simon, if you like?' said Bella, then glanced at the inspector before adding, 'On the sofa.'

'No thanks, Bella,' her friend replied. 'If I don't go back tonight, I'll never face it.'

****

A few hours later the inspector delivered Simon to his house, and the three of them went in together, to make sure that the young man could cope with staying there that night. Bella wasn't sure that it was the inspector's responsibility to check such things, but she'd already realised how kind he could be.

He insisted on driving Bella back to her flat too and they chatted companionably on the journey.

'What you mentioned last night, about your ambitions,' the inspector said awkwardly as he parked outside her flat, 'Joining the police force. You should do it!'

'Thanks, but I missed the boat on that one,' said Bella, 'Besides, there's nothing wrong with working in a teashop.'

'No, there isn't,' he agreed, 'But is it really what you want to do for the rest of your life? It seems a waste to me.'

'Oh, so you think I'd be better off working for some old dinosaur like you?'

'Something like that,' said the inspector. 'Think about it. I'm sure it's still a possibility. After all the help you've given me on this case, I'd be happy to put you forward.'

'No thanks,' she replied. 'I don't want anyone pulling strings for me.'

'That's not what I mean,' Blake answered, embarrassed. 'Just that if you wanted to apply, I'd be happy to write you a reference. You've proved your abilities, over the last couple of days ... and we need people who are clever and resourceful and good in a crisis.'

Bella got out of the car and headed for her front door.

'At least think about it!' he called. 'You've got my number.'

'Numbers can be deleted,' she teased, letting herself in and shutting the door behind her.

She glanced at her phone and pulled up the inspector's number, tempted to delete it just because she didn't like hm interfering in her life. Then she shrugged and tucked it back in her pocket.

'Numbers can be deleted anytime,' she said to herself. 'It doesn't have to be right now!'

****

A Note from the Author

This book went to print in April 2020 and was due to launch at Geek Camp that month, but the Corona virus hit, and life changed for all of us. No Geek Camp, No Conventions, No Cosplay, No Shows.

If you're reading this and have time (and money) to spare, please buy a book by one of the authors listed in these pages (some of whom sell most of their books at events and conventions).

For the performers among us, all work stopped dead, but you can buy CDs or downloads from some of the bands, go to their gigs when the world turns again, or consider booking them if you organise an event.

Supports the Arts, even in lockdown, so that we can still be there for you in the future.

Authors

Here is a little information about each of the authors mentioned in the book. I'm not going to attempt to list every work that they've produced but I'll try to give a taster of each writer. *(Comments in italics are purely my opinions and recommendations.)*

Samantha Lee Howe/Sam Stone

Samantha Lee Howe began her professional writing career in 2007 and has been working as a freelance writer for small, medium and large publishers, predominately writing horror and fantasy under the pen name Sam Stone. Samantha lives in Lincolnshire with her husband David and their two cats. Her Steampunk books are The Kat Lightfoot series.

Zombies at Tiffany's (Kat Lightfoot Book 1) Kat Lightfoot thought that getting a job at the famed Tiffany's store in New York would be the end of her problems. She has money, new friends, and there's even an inventor working there who develops new weapons from clockwork, and who cuts diamonds with a strange powered light. This is 1862, after all, and such things are the wonder of the age. But then events take a turn for the worse: men and women wander the streets talking of 'the darkness'; and random, bloody attacks on innocent people take place in broad daylight.

This is the series Artie is fan of. *It's a great mix of characters, action, and zombies...all in a steampunk world set during the American Civil War.*

Among her many other works are *Posing for Picasso* - a supernatural thriller. This is an unusual cross-over between supernatural fiction and a detective story. *It's imaginative and intriguing.* She has also had a new novel, a thriller called The Stranger in Our Bed, published by HarperCollins recently. Find out more at www.samanthaleehowe.co.uk

David J Howe

David J Howe has been involved with Doctor Who research and writing for over thirty years. He has been consultant to a large number of publishers and manufacturers for their Doctor Who lines, and is author or co-author of over thirty factual titles associated with the show, including *The Target Book*. He also has one of the largest collections of Doctor Who merchandise in the world! He is Editorial Director of Telos Publishing Ltd and has also written a novelisation:

Daemos Rising: Kate Lethbridge-Stewart is summoned by an old friend, Douglas Cavendish, to help him with a problem he has with ghosts and voices in his head. Aided by a time-traveller from the future, Kate must outwit both the ancient race of Daemons, and the Sodality, a human cult-like organisation from the future, which is intent on gaining control over time. It spins off from the 1971 BBC Doctor Who adventure 'The Daemons'.

Jamie is chatting to David about this one. *It has a wonderfully eerie feel and is very atmospheric.*

Robert Harkess/R B Harkess

He used to work with computers and boss people about to earn a crust. Now he spends most of his time writing, usually Science Fiction or Steampunk, and running around the country to various conventions and other events where he can peddle his books and meet new - and returning - readers. He lives in Lincolnshire, England, with a wonderful partner and two attention-seeking dragons shape-shifted into the forms of conventional felines.

Underland (Warrior Stone Book 1) is a twisted copy of our world that uses industrialised magic to power ancient stolen technology. Claire Stone accidentally slips through a crack between the worlds, and meets Evie, a girl about her own age, chasing a Morph. Things go wrong and Claire ends up rescuing Evie, and does so well she is offered a job as a Warrior, hunting down and destroying the shape shifting beasts. Who could say no?

This is the book that Jess starts to read to Alec in hospital. *It's a great mix of Steampunk and Magic.*

Also available is the sequel *White Magic*, and *Keene and the Last Guardian*, both of which are in the Steampunk Genre. For his Science Fiction works please visit his website

www.robertharkess.co.uk

Lauren K Nixon

An ex-archaeologist enjoying life in the slow lane, Lauren K Nixon is an indie author fascinated by everyday magic. She is a member of a team of consultant proof-readers and ghost writers working for Coleman Editing, providing freelance copy-editing services for aspiring writers.

Lauren is the author of numerous short stories as well as *The Fox and The Fool*, *Mayflies*, and *The Chambers Magic* series. She also curates the fabulous short story Superstars, a vibrant community of writers, whose anthologies are now available.

The House of Vines (Chambers Magic Volume 1) At the heart of the sleepy market town of Brindleford is an old shopping arcade. Half-empty and generally overlooked by the inhabitants, it is full of secrets. But there are darker things afoot; in a church on the outskirts of the town an ancient evil is stirring. Christopher Porter thought he knew what to expect from life: not a great deal, having been bitten by a werewolf. Now, all he wants is a normal life. Ivy Burwell is the last in a long line of witches and trying her hardest to avoid her destiny. It won't be easy, with the owners of a magical bookshop, a grumpy poltergeist, two orphaned runaways, a redoubtable florist, a retired music teacher (and his heavily pregnant Labrador), several unsavoury wizards, a lithographer, a necromancer with a grudge, a horde of Technomancers and a half-Troll getting in the way! Oh, and a parrot.

This is the doorstop of a book that she sells to Katy. *It's a terrific read, every single page of it.*

Simon Henderson

He's been dreaming of writing children's books for many years, Now he's finally achieved it, and he wants to help children learn to read.

Norman the Snail and the Climb: This first story describes the efforts of a little snail that wants to explore his dreams and reach the sky. It was written to show that no matter how small you are, or how big your dreams might be, there is nothing to stop you chasing your goals. With bright, colourful, illustrations by the talented Bazmac this is a delightful tale for children of all ages.

Coming soon *Captain Cold Blood* which is in development with illustrator: J. S. Augustin

Artie chats to this author in the book. *It's a charming tale for younger children.*

The Herod Family

Tracey, her husband Mick and daughter Caitlin are the backbone of The Book Base (or Author Central in real life). Without them the books wouldn't be sold, and the authors looked after, as we are running around from panel to panel and someone has to hold the whole thing together. *You will be pleased to know that Caitlin suffered no actual damage from her virtual burns.*

Fiona Angwin

I was born and brought up on the Wirral Peninsula and have been addicted to books, animals and theatre since I was a child. This has led to a rather varied career. I did a Zoology degree at Liverpool University, followed by drama training, and have juggled acting, writing, directing, theatre administration, being a bat worker and environmental educationalist, and working as a zookeeper/presenter at Chester Zoo for a couple of years. As well as the published works listed here, I've written a number of plays and musicals for the theatre companies I've worked with. I'm currently working as The Yarn Spinner - storyteller and puppeteer (see www.theyarnspinner.com) This involves building many of the unique puppets I need (see: www.touchstonepuppets.com)

I also perform a geeky sci-fi puppet show, *Behind the Sofa*, at conventions and events. To see a video montage, go to

http://youtu.be/VH13LKuVHdw

Soul-Lights: When thirteen students at a party hold a séance just for a laugh, they have no idea of the terrifying consequences, unleashing evil across the city. By the end of the week, one of them will be dead, another as good as, and a third will have lost their soul. Their only hope is a probationary guardian angel, Thren, who's been sent to look after them as a punishment for his bad attitude, and his prim and proper mentor, Tor. Time is running out for the students and only Thren can save them. The question is can he be bothered? Soul-lights is a sparkling, darkly comic tale of angels and demons, students, warring clergy and the walking dead, set in the cathedral, university, zoo and historic city of Chester!

Soul-Scars: Three months after being attacked by a demon, the survivors of a group of students are still struggling to come to terms with what happened. However, Thren, their hopeless guardian angel, blames his own initial wisecracking and casual attitude for what went wrong. Not even Tor, his rather annoying fellow angel, can lift his spirits, especially as she's busy worrying about who her own charge,

Bex, is dating. Thren begins to go into meltdown while attempting to protect the whole of the City of Chester, and the students in particular, from danger, and things start to go wrong again. Demons find another way to come through from The Darkness, but this time the stakes are even higher...putting not just the students, but the whole world, at risk. Thren is discovering angels have feelings (who knew?) and it's killing him! Another darkly comic tale of angels, demons, imps and celestial consequences set in the historic city of Chester.

Hunted by Demons: (published by Telos Publishing) Phoebe and her fiancé, Marco are looking forward to the birth of their first child and their forthcoming wedding when tragedy strikes. During what appears to be a freak accident, Marco is killed. Phoebe is left alone and devastated but that is the least of her worries. Something is stalking Phoebe, and it won't stop until it has every drop of her blood. A tale of demons, angels and imps.

Manx Folk Tales: (published by The History Press.) These lively and entertaining folk tales are vividly retold by professional storyteller Fiona Angwin. Their origins lost in the oral tradition, these thirty stories from the Isle of Man reflect the wisdom (and eccentricities) of the Island and its people. Discover why the Manx cat has no tail and what makes the Loaghtan sheep so unusual. Read about the Black Dog of Peel, Jack the Giant Killer, the Buggane of St Trinians, fairy folk and the phynodderee. These enchanting tales will appeal to modern readers and storytellers, young and old alike, both on the Isle of Man and elsewhere.

If you've enjoyed this book, please leave a review on Amazon or/and Goodreads, let your friends know and share it on-line. It makes a massive difference to authors to have reviews.

Thank You!

Performers

A lot of what they do was described within the book, but I thought I'd add a little detail.

The Host – Adam Colclough

Rescued from an island in The Canaries where he was wowing the crowds, Adam now assists with just about anything and everything in the Area 51 office, as well as appearing on stage.

A chemistry graduate with a creative flair, Adam is just as much at home giving a Potions Class for a Harry Potter event in The Maldives as he is fronting and co-ordinating a circus sideshow at Glastonbury Festival. When he isn't beavering away at his desk in Area 51, he can be found dressed as his favourite alter-ego, The Joker from Bat Man! Manages   Jimcredible

Area 51 Directed by Matt Page - The Entertainment Team

Matt plots Area 51's course through the outer reaches of the entertainment universe, with energy, dedication and creativity. Area 51 is a major provider of interactive performers for events and parties of all sizes, supplying dancers, stilt-walkers, jugglers, magicians, musicians and more. Matt himself has a background in photography, journalism, cartooning and caricature creations, and was always destined for a career in arts and entertainment.

He oozes an incessant stream of brainstorming concepts and it's his imagination that helps sculpt the company's distinctive vibe.

Pop-Up Puppet Cinema
The best way to describe Pop-up Puppet Cinema is like Punch and Judy colliding with Hollywood. PPC condense classic films into live puppet shows, mocking the originals with plenty of warmth and admiration.

Jollyboat - Comedy Pirate Brothers
Jollyboat is a British musical comedy double act. Formed in Liverpool in 2010, and now based in London, the act comprises brothers Ed and Tommy Croft. They are known for their Pirate Pop Songs and Keyboard Love Songs. In 2011 Jollyboat won the Musical Comedy Awards at the Edinburgh Fringe Festival. Geeky musical comedian duo, touring the UK Anime + Comic-Con scene. *These were the two kind young men who tried to help Simon, but Ramilid dragged him away.*

Blues Harvest - The perfect sci-fi cantina band!
Blues Harvest have built up a most impressive reputation as the go-to party band for geek events, having played their blend of Star Wars parodies and other classic movie songs in comic-cons, space centres and cantinas across the galaxy.

Professor Elemental
Paul Alborough, professionally known as Professor Elemental, is a steampunk and chap hop musical artist. After being approached to do a concept album of hip-hop as it would sound in different time periods, Emcee Elemental created the character of Professor Elemental. While the album never came to fruition, the character stuck. Professor Elemental has since been seen performing as a solo act or in theatre acts such as Come into My Parlour. He is also popular at steampunk events.

Hats Off Gentlemen it's Adequate
Genre defying band combining prog/alt-rock and electronica, with elements of minimalism, funk, classical, acoustic, and metal. They are a small independent band, releasing music through their own nano-label (basically Malcom and his laptop). Their music often explores scientific themes, and doesn't follow a traditional pattern or path but rather evolves.

Malcolm Galloway - Vocals, guitar, keyboard, producer and Mark Gatland - Bass, keyboard, backing vocals, co-producer either on their own, or with Kathryn Thomas – flute, vocals

While Blake wasn't sure what to make of their music, I really enjoyed it! Give them a listen!

LevelUp Leroy
Geek Camp's regular DJ is LevelUp Leroy, who specialises in creating a super nerd-centric mix and mash-up between EDM, K-Pop, Chip Tune, Rock and the Top 40. *However, like Jess, I'm always too exhausted to stay until the end, so I couldn't really include him in any detail (Sorry Leroy), though Mel, Mike and Lee stay on for his set.*

The Dark Room created by John Robertson
The Dark Room is the world's only live-action videogame. And definitely the only live-action videogame to become an actual videogame. Interactive and insane, this is improv comedy and retro gaming fused into a deranged rock n'roll game show.

You Awake to Find Yourself in...THE DARK ROOM....

There are so many people I couldn't cram into this book without slowing the plot down:- Splendid moderators and interviewers like Simon 'Spindles' Potthast, Emma Potthast, Adele Wearing and Sara Smith to name just a few, as well as all the behind the scenes team at Chic Festivals who organise the overall event (Sci-Fi Weekender). You are all awesome! Please forgive the omissions and enjoy the book anyway.

Writers and Performers – Internet Links

Fiona Angwin:	www.theyarnspinner.com
	www.fionaangwin-writer.com
	Facebook.com/writerfionaangwin
	www.touchstonepippets.com
David J Howe:	howeswho.blogspot.com
Samantha Lee Howe:	www.samanthaleehowe.co.uk
Robert Harkess:	facebook.com/rbharkess
	Instagram.com/harkesswrites
Lauren K Nixon:	www.laurenknixon.com
Simon Henderson:	facebook.com/simonhendersonauthor
Adam Colclough:	facebook.com/jimcrediblecosplay
	adam@area51.co
Area 51:	www.area51.co
	matt@area51.co
PopUp Puppet Cinema:	www.popuppuppetcinema.co.uk
	Facebook.com/popuppuppetcinema
Blues Harvest:	andy.lyth@gmail.com
	www.blueharvet.co.uk
Professor Elemental:	professor-elemental@outlook.com
	www.professorelemental.com

Writers and Performers – Internet Links Continued

Jollyboat: www.jollyboat.co.uk

Hats Off Gentlemen: www.hatsoffgentlemen.com

LevelUp Leroy: www.levelupleroy.co.uk

The Dark Room: www.thejohnrobertson.com/thedarkroom

Dr Squee (Iain Shaw): www.facebook.com/The-Doctor-Squee-Show-100158314972609

Printed in Great Britain
by Amazon

10159469R00078